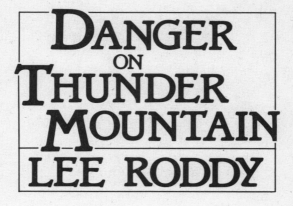

DANGER ON THUNDER MOUNTAIN

LEE RODDY

BETHANY HOUSE PUBLISHERS

MINNEAPOLIS, MINNESOTA 55438

A Division of Bethany Fellowship, Inc.

Published by Bethany House Publishers
A Division of Bethany Fellowship, Inc.
6820 Auto Club Road, Minneapolis, Minnesota 55438

Printed in the United States of America

Library of Congress Cataloging-in-Publication Data

Roddy, Lee. 1921–
    Danger on Thunder Mountain / Lee Roddy.
       p. cm. — (An American adventure series ; bk. 3)
    Summary: Joining her cousin Ruby on a search for Ruby's missing fa-
ther, leads Hildy to a confrontation with wealthy cattleman, Ozzie Kessick.
    1. Adventure and adventurers—Fiction. 2. Ranch life—Fiction.
    I. Title. II. Series: Roddy, Lee, 1921–
    American adventure series ; bk. 3.
PZ7.R6Dan   1989
[Fic]—dc20   89–18085
ISBN 1–55661–028–9   CIP

To our grandson,
Patrick O'Shaughnessy Roddy,
son of Steven L. and Katie O'Shaughnessy-Roddy,
for bringing us great joy
as our first grandchild.

AN AMERICAN ADVENTURE SERIES

LEE RODDY is a bestselling author and motivational speaker. Many of his over 48 books, such as *Grizzly Adams, Jesus, The Lincoln Conspiracy*, the *D. J. Dillon Adventure Series*, and the *Ladd Family Adventures* have been bestsellers, television programs, book club selections or have received special recognition. All of his books support traditional moral, spiritual, and family values.

CONTENTS

CHAPTER ONE

TROUBLE IN A GHOST TOWN

As Hildy Corrigan walked barefooted past the adobe brick ruins in the Mother Lode community called Simple Justice, she didn't know she was headed straight into trouble.

Gazing at a beautiful Victorian home on a tree-shaded hill, she hardly noticed the people who stared at her pet raccoon riding astride her neck. She looked longingly at the graceful old house. *Could this be the "forever home" of her dreams?* she wondered.

Suddenly she heard a man cry out, "Stop that! Leave me alone!"

Hildy whirled and glanced down the side street.

A short distance away a half-dozen boys surrounded a tall, slender, bareheaded man wearing faded hickory-striped overalls and scuffed cowboy boots.

The man lunged awkwardly toward a short, stocky boy. "Gimme back my hat!" he shouted.

The other boys laughed as the stocky kid waved a sweaty, tapered western hat just out of the man's reach.

"Here, take it, sheepherder!" the boy jeered, dancing away from the man's flailing arms.

The stocky boy, about fourteen, wore the typical ranch hand's blue denim shirt, pants, and pointed-toe boots. Rattles from a snake stuck up from the metal-studded black leather band of his cowboy hat.

The man staggered forward, reaching for his hat. His long, untidy blond hair fell on both sides of his unshaven face like hound dog ears. As his fingers almost touched the hat, the stocky boy tossed it to a skinny kid wearing gabardine knickers and knee-length hosiery. Turning to follow the hat, the man staggered and fell to his knees in the dusty street.

The boys' explosive laughter echoed off the surrounding low hills covered with scrub oak and digger pines.

Hildy's heart beat faster and she glanced behind her to see where her cousin was. Ruby Konning was apparently still looking at the old horse-drawn fire engine they had seen in the dark, musty-smelling building down the street. Hildy didn't blame her. The shade was welcome relief from the hot morning sun of mid-July, 1934.

Turning her attention back to the cruel boys, Hildy impulsively jumped off the high board sidewalk to the unpaved street and ran toward them. The raccoon astride her neck grabbed her long brown pigtails and hung on. Hildy's blue percale housedress flopped about her knees as she ran. Without a word she dashed over to the boy with the man's hat and snatched it away.

"Hey!" The boy spun to face her. "Give that back!"

Keeping her eyes on the boys, Hildy silently handed the hat to the man. She decided that the stocky boy was the leader. "Why don't you go play someplace else?" She propped her hands on her hips in a defiant stance.

The ringleader's hazel eyes opened wide at the sight of the raccoon. "Look, you guys! That's a coon on her neck!"

The boys quickly surrounded Hildy, talking excitedly and firing questions at Hildy about the masked animal. Out of the corner of her eye, Hildy noticed the tall stranger put on his hat and stagger around the corner out of sight.

"Where'd you get the coon?" the stocky boy demanded.

"Found it in a nest in a tree when it wasn't much past being weaned." The twelve-year-old girl felt relieved that the boys had apparently forgotten their antagonism toward her for interfering. "Her name's Mischief," Hildy added.

The stocky boy reached out suddenly and pulled the animal's ringed tail. Laying back its ears, the raccoon snarled and tried to scramble higher on Hildy's head. The boy laughed and again reached for the tail.

Hildy spun away. "Don't do that!"

"Who's going to stop me?"

Hildy's heart speeded up as the ring of boys tightened around her. "Yeah!" another boy shouted. "You messed up our fun with that drunk sheepherder, but you can't stop us from pestering that coon!"

Hildy reached up to steady Mischief as the frightened animal climbed on top of the girl's head. Hildy turned away, trying to stay out of the boys' reach.

The ringleader reached for the raccoon again. "Who are you, anyway?"

Hildy knocked his hand down just before it touched Mischief's tail. "I'm Hildy Corrigan from Lone River, down in the valley."

"A flatlander!" the stocky boy mocked. "And a sheepherder lover, too! Come on, you guys! Let's grab the coon!"

Before Hildy could reply or act, she heard her tomboy cousin's voice right behind her. "Y'all leave Hildy be, ye hear?" Ruby hollered. Also barefooted, a year older and an inch taller than Hildy, Ruby wore blue denim overalls and a shirt that hid a surprisingly strong body. She had biceps that many boys envied.

The stocky boy laughed. "Y'all?" He mimicked the definite Ozark accent. "Y'all Okies gonna make us?"

Ruby drew in her breath sharply.

Hildy whispered to her cousin, "Ruby, don't—"

It was too late. Ruby's arm shot out like a striking snake and knocked the cowboy hat off the stocky boy's head. Instantly, her hand closed on a handful of tousled sandy hair and yanked hard.

"Ow!" the startled boy cried. "Let go, you dumb girl!" Bending his head to ease the pain, he tried to swing at her, but she arched her body away and pulled his hair harder.

The other boys shouted encouragement to their ringleader as Hildy glanced from one angry face to another, trying to think of a way out of this predicament.

Ruby gritted her teeth. "Say uncle!"

The stocky kid looked up at her. "You know who I am?" he yelled.

"Shore do!" Ruby snapped. "Yore name's mud less'n ye say uncle real fast!"

"Wait'll I get my hands on you!" the boy shouted.

Then from behind the girls came a man's soft voice. "That's enough, Rob."

Hildy and Ruby spun around to see an older man wearing an olive drab army-style campaigner hat and full-cut breeches, an imitation of those worn by doughboys in France scarcely sixteen years before.

A circular box in the left pocket of his chambray work shirt indicated that he dipped snuff. His leather boots were laced to the knees with rawhide thongs. Hildy sensed this man was equally at home in town or on a ranch. He was certainly no working cowboy like her father. The man was probably a cattle rancher.

"Uncle Oz," the boy cried, "she's pulling my hair out by the roots!"

The man's soft voice came again. "Young lady, you can let go now."

Ruby looked at her cousin, who nodded. Releasing her hold, Ruby rubbed her greasy hand on her overalls. "Y'all do that agin, and I'll snatch ye plumb baldheaded—the lot of ye!"

The man glanced at the raccoon, then at the girls. "I'm Ozzell Kessick and this is my nephew, Rob," he said. "Why don't you girls step out of the sun with Rob and me? Then each of you can explain what this is all about. The rest of you boys go find something else to do."

A few minutes later, in the shade of a sagging wooden garage that apparently had been a stable at one time, the rancher listened without comment to Ruby's, Rob's, and Hildy's version of what had happened.

"I see," Kessick said at last. He gazed thoughtfully into the street.

Hildy followed his gaze. The tall man she had defended had vanished. Along the dusty street a couple of buckboards with horses were hitched to a rail, a Model T Ford stood at the curb, and an unattended gray burro made its way down the center of the street. The tiny, trim hooves kicked up small puffs of dust as the sleepy-looking burro passed before them.

Ozzell Kessick looked back at Hildy. "That same sheepherder comes to town once a month to spend his pay on liquor," he explained. "The boys always have a little fun with him. So by now he should know enough to stay away from here. This is cattle country. He knows that."

Hildy shook her head doubtfully. "He sort of looked like a cowboy—I mean he wore cowboy boots and a cowboy hat, anyway. But even if he is a sheepherder, that's no reason to pick on him! My daddy says a man's lucky to get any kind of job in this Depression."

The rancher removed his felt vet-style hat and rubbed his perspiring forehead against his right shirt sleeve. "You've got a smart daddy, Hildy, but that sheepherder isn't very bright. Every month he comes into town, and every month the boys pick on him. You'd think he'd learn."

"Yeah," Rob agreed. "Dumb sheepherder!"

Ruby doubled up her fists and stepped toward the stocky boy. "Sheepherding's honest work," she argued. "King David was once a shepherd boy. You insultin' the Bible? If ye air, y'all're goin' to git a knuckle sandwich!"

Rob stepped back in surprise.

His uncle reached out and lightly touched Ruby's shoulder. "That won't be necessary, young lady." He paused for a moment, studying the raccoon still astride Hildy's neck. "How'd you two get into town? Simple Justice is a long way from civilization."

Hildy smiled to herself at the mention of the town's name. Her dad had told her that it was named for the Gold Rush miners' way of promptly punishing criminals without court proceedings. These boys apparently had their own version of simple justice.

Hildy looked up into Mr. Kessick's face. "My father drove us up from Lone River. That's his car." She pointed to a 1927 Lexington Minuteman Six parked under a Catalpa tree about two blocks away.

Hildy's arm swept toward a wooden water tower beside the railroad tracks. Two sturdy wooden corrals stood side by side on the opposite side of the tracks across from the tower.

"He's a rider for the Woods Brothers' Ranches," she explained. "Hear the train coming? It's bringing about a thousand wild cows from Nevada. My daddy's going to help unload them into the corral and then into a truck. Then they'll be driven to where there's still some grass that hasn't turned brown."

Ruby nodded. "Her daddy—he's my Uncle Joe—said Hildy'n me could come into this here town and look around awhile. Hildy's a-studyin' how to git a 'forever' home and I'm a-lookin' fer—"

"What's a 'forever' home?" Rob broke in.

"It's a place where my family won't ever have to move again," Hildy explained.

Ruby continued, ". . . and I'm a-lookin' fer somebody." She dug into the bib pocket of her overalls and produced a sepia-tone snapshot. "Y'all ever see this here man?"

The rancher took the picture and glanced casually at it. His nephew stepped closer and looked down at the old photo. "Uncle Oz! That looks like—!"

"Not likely, Rob!" Kessick interrupted. Turning the snapshot over, the rancher read aloud the inscription. "Highpockets Konning, 1921."

Hildy's hopes rose. "You've seen him?"

Still holding the picture, Kessick half-closed his eyes and looked thoughtfully at both girls. "Taken thirteen years ago. Uh . . . why do you want to know?" he asked softly.

"That thar's a pi'tcher of my daddy!" Ruby exclaimed.

The rancher stiffened slightly and exchanged startled looks with his nephew. "You don't say!"

"Y'all ever seed him? Huh, mister?" Ruby persisted.

Ozzell Kessick handed the picture back to Ruby, then reached into his shirt pocket. Pulling out the round box of snuff, he pinched some between his thumb and forefinger.

Hildy caught an unpleasant whiff of the moist tobacco. She had seen enough men use it to know this wasn't the dry type of snuff some sniffed up their noses. The dipping tobacco was common among men who worked outdoors in dry grass or timber where fire was a danger in the summer.

Kessick placed the wad of tobacco between his lower front teeth and lip before answering. "Nope, Hildy. Can't say I have," he said. "Well, I hear the train slowing up. You'll likely want to watch the cattle being unloaded. Come on, Rob. See you girls later."

As the man and boy walked away, Hildy watched them thoughtfully. "Ruby, why do you think Mr. Kessick stopped Rob when he started to say who that picture looked like?"

Ruby gently patted the snapshot, now again in her bib overall. "Y'all think they done lied to us?"

Hildy stepped onto the high board sidewalk, and her cousin fell in beside her. As they headed toward the corrals, Hildy could hear the cattle bawling above the train's noises. "I got that feeling, but I can't think of any reason why Mr. Kessick would tell a lie over a picture."

"Ye reckon he done seed my daddy and lied 'bout it?"

"Why would he do that?"

"I dunno, Hildy. But they's somethin' strange a-goin' on with that thar man and his nephew."

Hildy glanced quickly over her shoulder and saw Kessick and his nephew turn away abruptly. "They were watching us, Ruby. I wonder why?"

Hildy had a feeling she and Ruby were in danger.

Chapter Two

A CLUE FOR RUBY

Hildy stroked Mischief's tail as she watched the train inch alongside the corrals made of stout peeled oak. She had never seen a train in the Ozark Mountains of Arkansas where she had lived until the month before. Then she and her family, with Ruby, had come to California, "the Promised Land." So far, it hadn't been that for the Corrigans, but everyone hoped things would improve. Hildy looked over at her cousin.

For the moment, Ruby had apparently forgotten the strange behavior of Ozzie Kessick and his nephew. Grinning broadly, she waved at the engineer in the cab. He doffed his pale blue-and-white-striped cap and smiled at her from the small open window.

Ruby turned to Hildy. "Didja ever see anythin' as purdy as a train en-gine with its bell a-clangin', its whistle a-blowin', and them silvery things a-flashin' back and forth in the sunlight, drivin' them thar big wheels?"

Hildy laughed at her cousin's enthusiasm. Setting aside her own questions about the rancher and his nephew, she watched the huge black engine stop with a hissing of steam and squeal of metal wheels on iron rails.

"Trains are special, all right," Hildy said. "But remember what my daddy warned about getting near those cows in the train cars—especially cows with calves. They're right off the Nevada range and wild as deer. So maybe we'd better climb up on the top of that truck cab so we'll be out of danger while we watch." She pointed to a stake-sided truck to the right of the corrals.

"I like that tree yonder better," Ruby replied, pointing. "See how the limb done growed right out over the first corral? A body couldn't ask fer no better seat'n that."

"If the limb broke, though, it'd pitch us right into the corral with all those horns and hooves. Mischief and I'll settle for the top of the truck."

"Suit yoreself!" Ruby started barefooted toward the corrals but stopped at the sight of a man on horseback leaving the shade of the tree and heading toward them. "Here comes yore pa!"

Joe Corrigan rode easily in the western saddle, reins lightly held in his left hand. His right hand reached up and tipped his gray wide-brimmed cowboy hat back from his blue eyes and deeply tanned square face. Hildy's father was a powerfully built man with faded blue jeans and sturdy denim shirt buttoned at the neck and wrists. His cowboy boots in the stirrups were caked with dried mud.

He reined in the big bay gelding with black points on the mane, tail, and lower legs. "You gals have any luck in town?" he asked.

Hildy and Ruby exchanged glances. This wasn't the time to talk about what had happened.

Ruby reached out and stroked the horse's coarse, black mane. "Nothin' much, Uncle Joe. Say, is this here yore famous cuttin' horse ye been a-tellin' about?"

"Best on the ranch," he assured her. "Name's Lucky. After Lucky Lindy."

Hildy felt a slight stir of emotion. She thought of her friend Spud and his dog, Lindy. Almost everybody had a dog, cat, mule, canary, or something named after Charles A. Lindbergh. Seven years before, he became the first aviator to fly nonstop from New York to Paris.

"Lucky Lindy" had so captured the world's adoration that it seemed the least people could do to honor Lindbergh was to name something after him, especially since his son had been kidnapped and murdered two years earlier. Spud's devotion to Lindbergh was so great that he named his Airedale Lindy, and the boy wore an aviator-style cap year-round.

Hildy's father continued telling about his mount. "This here's a mountain horse. Sixteen hands high. Big for a cutting horse. See how long his legs are? Most other riders have small cow ponies that can't keep up with Lucky. He's so strong and fast from being raised in the mountains that he can outdo any horse I've ever seen."

"Kin I ride him, Uncle Joe?" Ruby asked.

"'Fraid not. First time he made a sudden cut, he'd leave you sitting on nothing way up in the sky. You'd hurt right smart when you landed," he said with a laugh. "Keep an eye on him when we're working those cattle and you'll see what I mean. We've got to separate the cows with calves into this first corral." He pointed. "Cows without calves go into the other one."

Turning, he glanced at the slat-sided cattle cars. "Well, I see they're opening the doors. I'd better go help. Remember what I said, girls."

"We know," Ruby replied, repeating his warnings on the drive up from the valley to these foothills. "Stay away from them thar cows. They ain't never seed nothin' but jackrabbits, side-winders, an' sagebrush till they was rounded up fer shipment to here."

Joe Corrigan chuckled. "I don't think those were exactly my words, Ruby, but you got the facts right. These cattle probably never even saw a horse at a distance until a couple days ago. It's a cinch they never saw a person on foot. So don't you girls get near them, or they'll horn you—'specially a cow with a calf at her side."

Hildy petted her raccoon. "I'm going to take Mischief and climb up on the roof of that truck."

"Can't do that," her father replied. "That truck'll soon be loaded with cattle. You girls just better find a seat somewhere else." He reined Lucky around and headed for the train.

Hildy watched her father rejoin about ten other riders. The first cattle car's big side door slid open, and a mixture of long-horns and Herefords poured down a high-sided ramp into the corral.

Instantly, the ceaseless bawling of cattle filled the air along with the shouting and whistling of the riders. The dust swirled so thick that the girls could hardly breathe.

Ruby pointed to the tree again. "That don't leave us no choice but to set up thar. Ye a-comin'?"

Hildy considered the idea, then shook her head. "Mischief is getting restless. She's not sure what to make of all that noise. I'll find a good spot with her. You'd better stay with us."

"I ain't no scaredy-cat!" Ruby declared, running toward the tree.

Joe Corrigan's mount swung back sharply, one of the char-acteristics of a good cutting horse. Racing up to the girls, he stopped in a spray of dust. "I just realized you two are barefoot!" he called above the noise. "You can get lockjaw around a place like this, if you step on a nail or puncture your foot. We can't afford a doctor, you know. Maybe you could sit up on that empty boxcar on the siding, but don't fall off!"

The girls looked where he was pointing; then he whirled Lucky back toward the cows. The cousins walked toward the boxcar thirty yards away on a siding.

Hildy reached up to reassure the raccoon trying to climb on top of her head. "Ouch! Stop pulling my hair, Mischief! Here, I'll move you down in my arms so you'll feel safer."

Ruby reached over to help disentangle the coon's front paws from Hildy's hair. "Ye ever notice how much like a human hand that coon's forepaws are, Hildy? Long and slender and sorta like a baby's."

"I've read that a raccoon has the most sensitive forepaws of any animal around," Hildy answered. "A coon's smart, too. We're going to have a lot of fun watching Mischief grow up."

The girls came to the gravel bed beside the track spur leading to the empty boxcar. Although their feet were calloused, they stepped gingerly over the rough, sharp gravel.

Ruby changed the subject. "Didja see any house today that looks like the one yore a-lookin' fer?"

"Not really, but I'm in no hurry. Just getting ideas for now, but I'll find it someday."

Hildy had lost track of how many states she'd lived in since being born in a sharecropper's cabin. Her one burning desire was to have a "forever" home where the family would never have to move again. But as long as the Depression lasted, there was always the threat her footloose father would go off to another state looking for work.

"I 'speck ye will," Ruby said, "but I'm not so shore I'll ever find my daddy."

"You'll find him," Hildy assured her with a conviction she didn't feel. "Just like I'll find our 'forever' home. Now, let's climb up on this car so's I can put Mischief down a while. She's getting harder and harder to handle."

Hildy started to pull herself up on the iron steps anchored to the end of the boxcar. Just then out of the corner of her eye, she caught a movement down the street. She glanced toward town. "Look!" she exclaimed. "Mr. Kessick's coming this way."

"What d'ye reckon he wants?"

"I don't know, but there's something about him and his nephew that I don't trust."

The raccoon seemed to sense Hildy's feelings, for the animal made low growling sounds deep in its chest. "Easy, Mischief!" Hildy said. Stroking the raccoon's fur, she turned in the gravel roadbed to watch the rancher's approach.

Kessick reached the shade of the boxcar before speaking. Then he looked at Ruby and said, "I've been thinking about that picture you showed me. Could I take another look, please?"

Wordlessly, Ruby produced the snapshot and handed it to the cattleman.

Mischief braced her feet against Hildy's body while the rancher thoughtfully examined the picture.

"Maybe could be him," he mused, handing it back.

"Ye seed my daddy hereabout?" Ruby exclaimed.

"Can't say for sure, young lady. That snapshot was taken several years ago, but it might be a fellow called Slim. I don't know his last name or even his real first name, but—"

"Whar is he?" Ruby interrupted.

"You might ask at the post office in Mushroom City." He pointed. "About a half-hour drive back toward the valley. Not far from where they're building that new dam at Thunder Mountain."

Ruby frowned. "Mushroom City ain't the town whar a woman at Grizzly Gulch tol' me my daddy was supposed to be goin', the last anybody knew. I mean, the place where I writ him care of gen'ral delivery at the post office he never answered." Her voice sounded more anxious. "Was this Slim married?"

Hildy struggled to hold Mischief still. The raccoon's back began to arch, and her fur rose along the neck as her ears laid down flat against her head. Hildy had seen dogs do similar things when they were frightened or angry.

The rancher glanced down at the raccoon, then at Ruby. "I didn't know Slim personally. Just saw him buckarooing around. He was tall and slender, like the man in your snapshot. Since that was taken thirteen years ago, it might be this same High-pockets Konning you're looking for. I thought you might like to check it out." Kessick touched the brim of his hat and walked away.

Hildy shifted the restless raccoon to another position in her arms. "Easy, Mischief, easy! The man's not going to hurt you."

Hildy glanced at her cousin and saw hope springing into Ruby's eyes. Hildy didn't want to discourage Ruby, but Ozzie Kessick and his nephew gave Hildy an uneasy feeling, too.

She looked toward her father just as half a dozen cows with calves bunched together and broke through the chute, pouring into the open, barren land around the corral. Hildy caught her breath as her father yelled and tried to head them off. The horse obeyed unspoken commands from Joe Corrigan's knees and his shifting weight in the saddle.

The cutting horse kept his hind legs tucked well under him

so he pivoted easily right or left while his front legs shot out in front. He seemed to be almost dancing as he anticipated heading off any animal that tried to bolt.

Ruby watched the scene calmly. "We could ask yore daddy to stop at Mushroom City on the way back down to Lone River."

Hildy shook her head but never took her eyes off her father. She knew he was in control, but she couldn't help but worry a little. "Daddy said it's going to be a sixteen-hour day, unloading those cows and then getting them into trucks. Riding's from sunup to sundown. That's why he had to give up his extra job of night janitor at the grammar school." She stroked Mischief reassuringly.

"Looks like Mischief don't trust that thar Mr. Kessick no more'n we do," Ruby said.

"What do you make of what he said, Ruby? You believe him?"

"Don't rightly believe I do, but . . . Watch out! Mischief's goin' to jump!"

The raccoon's body stiffened and her hind feet braced against Hildy's ribs. Hildy tried to hold Mischief, but the raccoon let out a squeal and launched herself into the air. Landing like a cat on all fours, she quickly waddled toward the tree trunk by the corral.

"Come back here!" Hildy called, chasing after the coon.

"Hildy, look out!"

Ruby's sharp cry made Hildy look up.

Two horned cows with calves broke away from those Lucky was herding back to the corral. The bellowing renegade cows bolted toward the raccoon.

Instantly, Lucky pivoted and quickly turned the nearest cow and calf back toward the herd. But the second cow lowered her horns and charged Mischief.

Hildy sprinted forward in a desperate race to reach her pet first. "Run, Mischief! Run!"

At the sound of the girl's voice, the cow and calf suddenly stopped. Glaring at Hildy, she bawled angrily, lowered her wicked horns, and thundered down upon the defenseless girl!

CHAPTER
THREE

A SURPRISE AT
THUNDER MOUNTAIN

For a moment Hildy froze in fear. Then she scooped the raccoon into her arms and frantically sprinted toward the corral. As in a nightmare, the cow's thundering hooves closed in fast from behind. Hildy could almost feel the animal's hot breath on her neck.

Ruby was screaming, but between the bawling and shouting inside the corral and the thick dust, none of the riders seemed to realize the dangerous situation Hildy was in. Then out of the corner of her eye, Hildy saw her father pivot Lucky toward her.

Hildy didn't dare look back as she neared the corral. Shifting Mischief to the crook of her arm, she clutched the coon close. It was risky jumping on the round oak rails with the wild Nevada range cows inside, but that seemed safer than getting gored from behind.

With Mischief struggling to get free from Hildy's tight grasp, the girl reached her other hand down and grabbed up her long skirt. She yanked it high above her knees so her legs would be free.

Letting go of the skirt, she reached out for the top corral railing and leaped as high as possible, skirt flying. As her fingers touched the top railing, her bare feet landed on the second corral pole from the bottom.

Hildy started to step up higher, but her left leg jerked violently. The bawling cow's long horn hooked upward. Hildy heard her dress tear. Panicking, she kicked free, bringing her leg up to a higher railing. She glanced down in horror. Had the horn done more than tear the dress? There was no sign of blood. No pain.

Bent almost double, hands and feet only about a foot apart, Hildy clutched the top rail while trying to control the struggling raccoon. There she perched precariously in momentary safety.

The cow below, with calf trailing every step, backed off and charged again. Hildy braced herself as the cow crashed into the sturdy corral. Hildy swayed with the impact but held on with one hand.

Mischief squealed in fright and tried to jump out of Hildy's arm. "Hold still!" Hildy cried above the noise and confusion. She could hardly see through the thick dust, but she heard the rapid thunder of Lucky's hooves. "Daddy's coming! Hold still, I said!"

Suddenly she could see him approaching, leaning low over the big mountain horse's neck, eyes wide with fear for her. His boot heels drummed hard against the gelding's flanks.

Hildy clutched the squirming raccoon tighter. "Just a moment longer and we'll be—" She looked inside the corral just in time to see several wild cows quickly turn together and charge toward her. "Oh! Oh!"

She glanced backward. The other cow was charging again, too!

"Oh no! If they all hit the fence together. . . !"

Hildy had only a couple of seconds to brace herself against the expected impact from both sides of the corral.

The cows inside the corral hit so hard Hildy almost lost her grip. Mischief's weight, added to the cows' impact, knocked Hildy off balance.

"Oh, noooo!" she shrieked, frantically trying to keep from falling into the corral while expecting the second blow from behind.

Suddenly, the cow outside spun away before hitting the fence. Lucky's big body shot between the cow and Hildy. The cow kicked high and ran off, trailed by her bawling calf.

Sitting far back on his haunches, the gelding slid to a stop. Joe Corrigan dropped the reins and reached up with both arms. "Jump, Hildy! Jump! I'll catch you!"

Letting go of the top rail, Hildy held on to the raccoon with both hands and started to jump. But just as she was about to push off with her feet, the cows—inside again—smashed into the corral. Hildy teetered on the railing and fell backward. Still clutching Mischief, she landed in her father's arms.

Joe Corrigan was breathing hard, his eyes full of fear. "You all right, Hildy?" He helped her settle in front of him in the saddle.

She took a sobbing, shuddering breath of relief as the cutting horse turned and began heading the renegade cow and calf back toward the corral gate.

"I . . . I think so." She glanced down at the raccoon. "We're both fine! Oh, Daddy! I was so scared. . . !"

"It's all right, honey! It's over! We'll be through here in another hour and we can head home."

"Home?" Hildy asked in surprise as he lowered her to the ground beside Ruby. "I thought it'd take all day?"

"Cattle inspector just showed up. Says the papers aren't in order. We can't unload any more until they are. Be tomorrow before that's done. So the boss is sending all us married riders home early."

Hildy and Ruby exchanged glances; then Hildy blurted, "Can we stop at a little town on the way down? Ruby's got a lead on the man who might be her daddy."

Joe Corrigan sat up straight in the saddle and glanced down at Ruby. "You have?" When she nodded, he added, "Then we'll check it out, by all means!"

It was nearly noon when the girls and Joe Corrigan got into

the Lexington touring car and headed toward Mushroom City. While they ate sandwiches from a pail that had once held lard, the cousins explained about their meeting with Ozzell Kessick and his nephew.

Hildy's father eased the car off the paved highway and onto the unpaved main street of Mushroom City. It did not live up to its name, which had been given in the Gold Rush. Now it was just another ghost town with less than a hundred people.

Mischief was asleep in the backseat when Mr. Corrigan parked in front of the adobe brick post office with iron shutters. The sturdy building materials had been the gold miners' ways of coping with the disastrous fires that often destroyed make-shift Mother Lode towns of canvas and wood.

Hildy approached the aging clerk at the grillwork window. "We're looking for a man called Slim," she said. "He's probably riding for some rancher around here. Looks like this. Show him, Ruby."

The clerk studied the snapshot through wire-rimmed glasses that barely perched on the end of his long nose. "Looks a mite like a feller I've seen. Can't say for sure, though," the clerk said, handing the picture back. "Anyway, he never got any mail, so I don't know his real name. Just saw him around town now and then."

Hildy's heart beat faster with hope. "You know where we can find him?"

"Cemetery in Reno, I 'spect."

"Cemetery?" Hildy and Ruby exclaimed together.

"Yep! Was rounding up some wild range cattle near there last month, I heard, when his horse throwed him. Died a couple days later."

Ruby let out a sobbing cry. "Daid? He cain't be!"

"Yes, he can, girlie. Is, too. I'm powerful sorry."

Back in the car, Ruby picked up Mischief and hugged her in a rocking motion and moaned in grief.

Hildy put her arm around her cousin and spoke softly. "Ruby, maybe shouldn't say this, but you don't know that this Slim was your father. Besides, I've been wondering if Ozzie

Kessick didn't already know this Slim was dead and sent us here on purpose."

Ruby looked up through red-rimmed eyes as Mischief squirmed away and crawled into Hildy's lap. "Why would he a-done that?"

"Maybe because he wants us to think your father is dead so you'll stop looking for him."

Ruby slowly straightened up and sniffed, rubbing the back of her hand across her nose. "If'n he done that a-purpose, it's 'bout the meanest, lowdown thing I ever heerd 'bout! But what possible reason could a body have fer doin' such a turrible thing?"

"It's only a wild hunch, but maybe Mr. Kessick really did recognize the man in your picture and doesn't want you to find him."

"I still don't see why—"

"Neither do I!" Hildy interrupted, "but I just wouldn't take anybody's word that your father's dead until we know a whole lot more than we do now."

Ruby pulled out the snapshot and looked at it thoughtfully. "I don't rightly know fer sure that this here is my pa! Ever'body back home in the Ozarks said I'm a woods colt—'specially yore mean old granny! They said I ain't got no pa a-tall."

Hildy knew all that, but she sensed her cousin's need to tell the story.

"My grandma raised me after Ma died when I was a baby. She was almost as mean to me as yore granny." Hildy's and Ruby's grandmothers were sisters but they never spoke.

Ruby continued, still fighting her emotions. "Some folks said my pa died shortly before I was born—died from bein' pizened by mustard gas in France! But what's the truth o' the matter? All these years of people a-pickin' on me fer somethin' I didn't have no say about! I'd jist like to know fer shore if'n he was alive or daid, or if'n it's true that I never had no pa, legal-like, I mean."

Hildy patted her cousin's arm reassuringly. "I don't want to make things worse for you, Ruby, but remember how you got that snapshot?"

"Shore do! Mrs. Witt done give it to me when we was a-tryin' to find yore stepmother and the kids after Molly done run off and left you! We followed their trail to Oklahoma where Molly's brother was a-workin' for the Witts. They said this here feller"— she tapped the photo—"done rode fer them some years back. But the name on the back, 'Highpockets' Konning, made them think maybe it was my pa on accounta our last names being the same. So they gimme this pi'tcher."

"Which I think Mr. Kessick and his nephew recognized," Hildy said with a little more conviction. "Maybe your father really is alive. You helped me find my family, so I'll help you find yours."

"Maybe I really ain't got none a-tall."

"But you won't know for sure if you don't keep looking! Please, Ruby! Don't give up yet!"

Joe Corrigan glanced over his shoulder at the girls in the backseat. "Won't do any harm to keep asking around, Ruby," he said. "Fact is, since we got some time, why don't we ask at other post offices on the way back to Lone River?"

Ruby liked the idea. As they headed home, they inquired at two other tiny towns without success. At the third, called Shaw's Ferry, which was located on the river by the highway, the tall postal clerk looked at the snapshot as the others had done. A slightly older clerk was loading mail sacks into a truck at the back door.

The tall clerk shook his head. "I don't know nobody called Slim or Highpockets Konning." He pushed a green eyeshade back from his freckled forehead. "But there're so many strangers in town since they started building the Thunder Mountain Dam near here that it's hard to know everybody anymore."

Ruby looked at Hildy and Joe Corrigan and sighed. "Well, thankee jist the same, mister," she said.

As they reached the car where Mischief was still asleep, the other clerk came running out of the post office, waving a letter. "Hey, folks!" he called.

They stopped and turned around.

"I overheard your questions inside and got to thinking that

name sounded vaguely familiar. After you left the window, I remembered we'd been holding a general delivery letter for a fellow named Nate Konning. It's unclaimed. Been here some time now."

Ruby reached out and took the letter. "I reco'nize it! It's the one I done writ after that lady in Grizzly Gulch gave me his last-known address. But I didn't send it to this town."

The clerk nodded and reclaimed the letter. "I know. It was forwarded here. Likely somebody where you sent it believed this Konning fellow had moved to Shaw's Ferry. So they sent it on, figuring he'd claim it here sooner or later."

Ruby's voice sounded anxious. "Y'all ain't a-joshin' me, air ye, mister?"

The clerk shook his head. "This letter wasn't forwarded without good reason."

Ruby's hazel eyes softened and she spoke wistfully. "Then maybe one day he'll come checking for mail, and y'all will give him this here letter o' mine! Then he'll know where to find me!"

The postal clerk snapped his fingers. "Hey! I just remembered! I was in the grocery store a few days ago when I heard someone talking about a man who bought a small ranch outside of town. I didn't pay that much attention to the name, but—"

"His name was Konning!" Joe Corrigan guessed. "Right?"

"That's right, mister!"

Ruby looked up. "Whereabouts is this ranch yore a-talkin' 'bout?"

"Right up against Thunder Mountain," the clerk replied. "Better come inside and I'll draw you a map. Otherwise, you're liable to get off on a side road where they're dynamiting for that new dam. Don't want you to get hurt."

A couple of minutes later, Hildy, her father, and Ruby watched as the postal clerk started his penciled drawing.

"This area is in the middle of something that looks like the letter *H*," the man began. He drew rapidly, explaining each stroke. "The left side or bar is Lone River."

"We live near Lone River," Hildy said.

The clerk nodded. "Your town takes its name from this river

that I'm showing you here. It starts in the high Sierras and runs down through these foothills to the valley, passing your town on the north.

"The right side of the *H* I'm drawing is about twenty miles south of here. That's the Tres Piedras River. It means Three Rocks in Spanish. And it's being dammed just above the town called Crane's Crossing. Thunder Mountain Dam is upstream in the canyon."

Ruby frowned. "That thar don't look like no *H* to me, mister," she protested.

"It does if I draw a line between the two upright bars—the rivers—like this. See?"

The three nodded as the clerk sketched a large oblong area between the two rivers and rapidly shaded it in with the pencil. "This is the cross bar on the *H*, which is Thunder Mountain. It's a flat topped-mesa of volcanic origin. We're here, just to the north of where it ends."

"Vol-canic?" Ruby asked. "What's that mean?"

"Countless ages ago," the clerk explained, "this area of California was part of a great volcano. Most evidence of this is gone, except here." He tapped the map.

"That's Thunder Mountain," he said. "It's eighteen miles long and nearly three miles wide. It's set almost due north and south between the rivers and rises five hundred feet or so above the road. It's almost like an old castle—walls straight up."

Hildy and Ruby exchanged wide-eyed glances.

"Once that was the lowest part, not the highest," the clerk continued. "It was an ancient riverbed that filled with hot lava. Over countless centuries, erosion took all the soft stuff. Now only this flat-topped mountain remains."

Hildy leaned forward. "Why's it called Thunder Mountain?" she asked.

"The Miwuk Indian legends claimed it was where the thunder hid when it wasn't rolling across the countryside. An irrigation dam was started near the south end to hold back Sierra Nevada Mountain snow melt for valley ranchers to water their crops in summer. That's called Thunder Mountain Dam."

The clerk tapped the map. "The ranch you want is right smack dab against the mountain. Can't miss it because it's the only cut, or passage, through that whole volcanic mass. In fact, it's called The Pass."

"Much obliged, mister," Joe Corrigan said.

The clerk handed the map to Hildy's father. "That's mighty valuable ranch property even though it's small," he said. "You see, for years, cattlemen drove their stock through that pass. Then Konning bought it and fenced it. Now drovers have to go around either end of the mountain. Made some of them mighty mad, I can tell you!"

"I suppose so." Joe Corrigan smiled faintly.

"One more thing," the clerk added. "I hear the ranch house is a kind of dugout, more like a Kansas sod house. It's low down in the ground, not standing high like a regular house."

"We'll find it," Hildy's father said. "Thanks again."

A little while later as dusk settled over the foothills, Joe Corrigan switched on the car headlights. He turned the Lexington Minuteman off the county gravel road onto a rutted dirt one.

From the backseat, both girls leaned forward and peered eagerly through the windshield. Mischief seemed to sense their anxiety and stood on his hind legs to look, too. Thunder Mountain loomed massively before them like an ancient castle, black and threatening.

As the car bounced and jarred slowly toward a narrow shaft of light that marked the pass through the mountain, Ruby grabbed Hildy's arm. "Kinda skeery-lookin', ain't it?" she mused.

Joe Corrigan laughed. "Don't let your imagination run away with you, Ruby," he said.

"I don't like it, nohow," she replied. "Oh, lookee yonder! I see a new barn! And over thar to the right—ain't that smoke?"

Hildy strained to see in the Lexington's headlights. "It's smoke, but it's coming up from the ground!"

Her father chuckled. "Not the ground, honey. That's a sod house. I've seen a few in my travels."

"The smoke's from a chimb'ny!" Ruby exclaimed. "That

means he's home! I'm a-gonna see him this blesset minute!"

Hildy impulsively hugged her cousin. "Oh, I hope so! But remember, we're not sure it's really your father."

"I'm shore," Ruby said. "It's jist got to be!"

"Barb' wire strung across the pass," Mr. Corrigan said. "Sign there, too: Cut Wire, Get Shot. See it?"

Hildy nodded and pointed. "Look! Somebody's moving over there by the smoke."

In the headlights, several figures popped up from an opening in the ground. "They're kids!" Hildy exclaimed. "Lots of them! And there's a woman, too."

Ruby let out a howl. "My daddy's done remarried! That must be his wife and chillern! Oh, I never expected no sucha thing!"

CHAPTER FOUR

THE SQUATTERS

In the light of the car's headlights the woman's face looked like the saddest, most discouraged face Hildy had ever seen. The deep lines of pain and despair startled the girl.

The woman was as skinny as a piece of baling wire, and her patched, faded dress flopped about her legs as she shuffled barefooted through the dust. Rimless eyeglasses perched on the end of her nose, and her untidy hair fell down over her eyes.

Four barefoot kids, about two to ten years old, trailed behind her. The oldest, a boy, wore ragged overalls with both knees worn through. Three tousled-haired, dirty-faced girls in dresses that were little more than rags, huddled close together. The youngest carried an empty Coca–Cola bottle with a nipple on top.

The woman walked over to the driver's side of the Corrigans' touring car and ducked her head to peer into the dark interior. "Howdy, mister," she said in a sad, weary voice. "Reckon ye done come to throw us off."

"Mrs. Konning?" Joe Corrigan asked uncertainly.

"I'm Mrs. Benton. Black widder spider kilt muh husbun' when we was a-hidin' in the cellar from the dust storms. The bank took the farm, or what was left sticking up out of the sand. Me'n the young'uns started out fer Californy, a-lookin' fer work."

The words poured out of the woman in an endless stream. "Got this far; then our ol' car broke down. Sold some parts fer food. Slept in the car couple nights, then got us a Hoovercart tow to here."

Hildy had heard of Hoovercarts. That was what people called a car pulled by a horse. Most Americans blamed former President Herbert Hoover for the Depression. He'd been voted out of office the year before and Franklin D. Roosevelt now occupied the White House.

The widow's gush of words continued. "We didn't see nobody aroun', and we was desprit fer a place to stay. Figgered it were a line shack fer riders. Anyways, it weren't locked ner nothin', so we stayed. Ain't hurt yore place none, mister. We'll git gone come daylight, though I ain't got the foggiest notion of where we'll squat next."

Hildy had never heard such a torrent of words, yet all this time the children hadn't said a word. After taking one look at the two girls in the backseat, they focused their full attention on the raccoon.

When the woman stopped to take a breath, Joe Corrigan took the opportunity to speak. "You're not Mrs. Nate Konning?" he asked.

"Tol' ye straight out, mister. I'm—"

"Where's my daddy?" Ruby interrupted from the backseat.

The tired, sad face leaned closer to the girls and the raccoon. "Yore daddy?"

"Nate Konning!" Ruby said emphatically. "This is his place, ain't it?"

"Reckon so, child, but ain't been no man around since we squatted here some weeks back. Less'n ye count them night riders that threatened us—"

Joe Corrigan broke in. "Excuse me, Mrs. Benton, but there's some confusion here. Mind if we step out and talk?"

"Be mighty proud to make yore acquaintance, but they's not

enough cheers ner benches inside for ever'body—"

"We'll stand," Hildy's father said, slipping out of the car to introduce himself, Hildy and Ruby.

"Hildy, hold on to your pet."

In the hulking shadow of Thunder Mountain, the widow lit a kerosene lantern and set it on an upturned garbage can, then introduced her children—Jacob, ten; Rachel, seven; Rhonda, four; and Becky, nearly two.

Hildy listened as their mother talked on, nonstop, about stringing ropes from their Kansas farmhouse to the well, barn, and outhouse. "That was so none of us got lost when them devil sand storms come up," she explained. "But one night, in the storm cellar amongst the jars I'd canned two seasons before, and with the grit in our teeth and our eyes stuck shut from the mud the tears made of the sand, my husbun' got bit on the neck and . . ." She shrugged and fell silent.

Hildy's heart went out to the children. Looking past their dirty faces and skinny, hungry bodies, she saw the softness deep in their eyes. "You want to pet my coon?" she asked.

Shyly, the kids gathered around in the pale yellow light of the lantern and gently stroked Mischief. The raccoon made chirring sounds and rubbed her masked face under the little hands.

Ruby watched the children for a moment and then looked up at their mother. "How'd ye know this here place belongs to Nate Konning?" she asked.

"Well, after we squatted here quite a spell and nary a living soul came near, I got to fearin'. I was afeerd I'd git throwed in jail fer trespassin' an' my kids'd starve. So I went to the Monitor County Courthouse at Hardrock one day an' looked it up. Nathaniel Konning bought this place, but there's a mortgage on it."

Hildy straightened up so suddenly that Mischief scrambled to grab on to the front of her dress. "Mortgage?" she repeated.

"Comes due August tenth," the woman said.

Ruby frowned. "Ain't today July twelfth? Then that's less'n a month away!" she exclaimed.

"I checked it careful," the widow replied. "Payment in full

has got to be made by four fifty-nine P.M. I noticed 'cause it seemed like a funny time. I reckon that's 'cause the courthouse closes at five o'clock."

Hildy's mind raced with an idea. "Who holds the mortgage?" she asked sharply.

"I'm plumb sorry to say I didn't notice," the widow replied. Taking a deep breath, she plunged into one of her avalanches of words. "Me'n the kids don't walk to town often, so it was a kinda excitin' day. I mean, we don't git much news out here, ye know. No radio or newspaper or nothin'."

Hildy's family didn't have a radio either, and the only newspapers or magazines they saw were those given by friends better off financially than the Corrigans.

Mrs. Benton raced on. "It were wonnerful a-hearin' things on radios in the stores an' readin' in *The Sacramento Bee* about what's goin' on—like the strike in San Francisco and that Actin' Governor Merriam a-callin' out the National Guard 'cause of the riots. We heerd that all the county sheriffs an' the highway patrol are protectin' growers' truck convoys while they's tryin' to git their peaches and things to market."

A smile flickered across her tired face. "That little Shirley Temple is showin' at the talkies in town," she continued. "An' Japan couldn't get President Roosevelt to nee-go-tiate a non-aggression pact like they wanted. Ye reckon we could git into a war with them if we don't work somethin' out, huh, mister?"

Joe Corrigan said he didn't know about such things.

Hildy had the feeling that Mrs. Benton was starved for somebody to talk with. But Hildy's mind was working on an idea. "Isn't it true that if the money's not paid on time, no matter who holds the mortgage, that person can foreclose and take the place?"

"That's what they done to us back home," the woman replied.

Hildy's father nodded. "That's the way it works. Somebody loans money and takes the property as what they call collateral. It protects the person or bank who lends the money."

Stroking Mischief's fur, Hildy turned to Ruby to see if she

understood the explanation, but her cousin seemed preoccupied.

"Missus Benton," Ruby began. "Ye ever see any personal things that belong to Nate Konning? Pi'tchers, old letters . . . things like that?"

The boy spoke for the first time. "They's a pi'tcher of a woman. Remember, Mama?"

"A woman?" Ruby's voice rose in excitement. "Can I see it?"

"Reckon so. Jacob, y'all run and fetch it. I'll show these folks 'round the place."

The boy took off running, and Hildy and Ruby exchanged understanding glances as the woman picked up the lantern and started walking toward the barn. "No well dug yet, so we git what little water we kin from a crick," the widow told them. "It runs along the base here."

Mrs. Benton looked up at Thunder Mountain rising straight above them like the battlements of a European castle. "Daytimes, in the distance, we hear them a-blastin' with dynamite, a-buildin' that there dam. Sometimes I'm afeered me'n the young'uns'll be buried alive, but we got nowheres else to go. 'Sides, if'n we're a-gonna die, nobody in town'd have to take up a collection to bury us."

Hildy reached out and touched the widow's arm. "You'll be all right," Hildy whispered. She liked this woman in spite of her gushy way of speaking. Hildy wanted to help but didn't know how. Mischief made a little chirring sound in the girl's arms. "See? Even my raccoon says so."

"Thankee kindly, Hildy," the woman replied. "Like ever'-body else in these hard times, we'll git by, somehows. Always do."

The woman turned back to Joe Corrigan. "We had us a right good scare shortly after movin' in here. Some riders come one night and tried to cut the barb' wahr thar. I lit me a lamp and they soon skedaddled."

She took a quick breath. "But a few nights ago, some riders come back—maybe the same ones as before—and yelled out as how they was a-gonna burn us out," she said. "Me'n the kids was too scared to answer, so we just hunkered down inside the house till they rode away. But I reckon they'll be back." Mrs. Benton seemed to have accepted that possible tragedy as just another in a series of them.

Mrs. Benton continued on, explaining that the barn must have been important to the owner because he had built it before he built a house. The barn wasn't big, but Hildy saw that it was sturdy and meant to last. But where was Nate Konning? And why hadn't he been around—especially if he was about to lose the ranch to foreclosure?

Just then Jacob came running back with the snapshot. Breathlessly, he handed it to his mother, and she held it close to the light for the visitors to see.

Ruby took one look and gasped. "That thar's my ma! My granny's got a pi'tcher 'zackly like that back in the Ozarks. When Hildy'n me took off sudden-like from there, I clean fergot to take it along."

Ruby spun to grab Hildy by the arms. "That means fer shore that Nate Konning is my very own daddy! We've found him! We've found him!"

Hildy didn't know what to say.

Her father cleared his throat. "Not quite, Ruby," he said, stepping into the lantern light. "We haven't quite found him yet, but we'd better do it inside of a month, or he'll lose this place!"

Mrs. Benton pushed her glasses up on her nose. "I was a-thinkin' he was probably daid until I seen yore lights a-drivin' up. But maybe he railly is."

"Don't say that!" Ruby snapped. "He's alive! I know he is. And we'll find him, won't we, Hildy? We'll find him in time, too, huh?"

Hildy looked at her cousin's desperate face in the lantern light and remembered what had happened just the month before in the Ozarks. Hildy came home one day and learned that her stepmother had moved away without a word, taking the other kids with her. Not knowing where her father was, Hildy had started looking for Molly and the kids. And throughout the long search and the reconciliation, Ruby had stuck with her.

"We'll find him," Hildy assured her in a soft voice. "Somehow, someway, we'll do it—and on time!"

Ruby reached out to the widow. "Missus," she said, "kin I have this pi'tcher of my ma?"

"It's not mine to give. I'm turrible sorry, Ruby."

Hildy's heart ached for her cousin. Ruby had none of the things Hildy considered important, like a family that loved her. Ruby didn't even know whether she had a father. She had never achieved much and she never got to just play. All she had was a photograph that might be her father, but now she was being denied a picture of her dead mother. *I know Mrs. Benton is right, though,* Hildy thought. The snaphot belonged to Nate Konning. The woman had no right to give it away. Still, all those things made Hildy hurt, and she knew her cousin hurt even more.

The widow looked at Joe Corrigan. "Uh . . . could I speak with you alone?" she asked.

The cousins watched in puzzled silence while the two adults walked a few feet away. Hildy couldn't make out what they were saying, but when the adults returned, her father suggested that they head toward home.

As the Lexington Minuteman bounced down the dirt road away from the ranch, Hildy leaned over the front seat. "What'd Mrs. Benton say to you?" she asked.

"She was afraid of getting Ruby's hopes up if this *is* Nate's place and he's about to lose it," her father replied. "But she said the county clerk told her that when Nate filed the mortgage papers, he'd said something about not being able to make a living off the ranch for a while. So he was going to Mariposa to look for a temporary buckarooing job to pay off the loan."

"Mariposa?" Ruby asked. "Where's that?"

"Couple hours' ride south and east of Lone River."

"Then let's go look for him thar!" Ruby exclaimed.

"It's not that easy! I don't have the time or money for gasoline to drive down there. I'd lose my job."

Hildy reached out and patted Ruby's arm as she slumped back against the seat. "We'll find a way, somehow, Ruby."

Mr. Corrigan sighed. "Car's heating up," he said. "Must be low on water."

Stopping at the first service station along the highway near Shaw's Ferry, Joe Corrigan unscrewed the radiator cap. The girls sat in the backseat playing with Mischief.

Inside the station, a radio blared. "Armed convoys of growers guarded by sheriffs' deputies and the highway patrol reported no more shooting incidents on the state's roads as the San Francisco riots continue."

"Wish we had a radio," Hildy mused. "Mrs. Benton knew more about what's going on than—wait. Listen!"

Both girls tensed and sat up quickly, dumping Mischief onto the floorboard.

Ruby looked out into the night. "Sireens!" she exclaimed. "Lots of headlights! Cars an' trucks an' motorsickle poh-leecemen a-comin' down the highway! Must be one of them thar convoys—" She broke off suddenly at a sharp sound. "Was that a shot?"

"Backfire, maybe," Hildy replied.

Another explosion ripped the night air, then another. "Them's gunshots!" Ruby cried.

A rapid-fire series of shots confirmed her words.

"Girls, get down!" Joe Corrigan shouted from in front of the car. "Get down on the floorboard!"

Hildy and Ruby threw themselves face down on top of Mischief. The raccoon squealed.

"They're still a-shootin'!" Ruby whispered. "An' they're a-comin' this-a-way fast!"

Above the sirens and roar of engines, another shot rang out close by. Hildy heard her father fall against the car's radiator.

"Daddy!" she screamed. Leaping up, she tore out of the car into the night.

CHAPTER
FIVE

CRYING CAN WAIT

In the weak light of the service station's outside electric bulbs, Hildy saw her father face down on the ground by the Lexington's left front wheel.

"Daddy!" she cried, bending over him.

He reached up suddenly and pulled her down hard beside him. "I told you to get down inside the car!"

"But I heard the shots, and you fell. . . !"

"I hit the fender getting out of the way. Now stay down!" He raised his voice. "Ruby, you okay?"

"I'm . . . jist skeered!" came the quavering reply. "So's Mischief!"

"Keep your head down and hang on to that coon!" her uncle commanded.

Hildy crouched against the big wheel, her father's body between her and the passing convoy. She listened for more shots, but there were none. The sirens faded into the distance. All the motorcycles, trucks, and cars passed on except one.

Hildy cautiously raised her head. A highway patrolman in puttees stopped a short distance away and swung his leg over the motorcycle. Kicking the stand into place, he ran toward

Hildy and her father. "You two all right?"

"I think so," Joe Corrigan replied. He got to his feet and helped Hildy up. "What happened?"

"Somebody got trigger happy, I guess," the patrolman answered. "Everybody's so tense about these convoys into San Francisco that when one of the trucks backfired coming down the mountain, some yokel sheriff's deputy fired his gun. Then it seemed everybody was shooting." He took out a handkerchief and wiped his brow. "Blame fools! Shooting up the night and scaring decent folks half to death. You sure you're okay?"

"We're fine," Hildy said. She glanced toward the backseat. "So's my cousin and my pet coon."

"Well, I'd suggest you get home as soon as you can," the patrolman said. Adjusting his cap, he returned to his cycle. "Not that I expect any more trouble, but you never can tell."

"We're on our way, Officer!" Joe Corrigan said.

When they reached the barn-house where the Corrigans lived, Hildy's three younger sisters and their stepmother rushed out to meet them.

Molly carried baby Joey in her arms. "Oh, Joe!" she exclaimed. "You were gone so long, we were worried! No telephone! No way to know where you were . . ."

Joe Corrigan scooped his three little girls in his one arm while encircling his wife's shoulders in the other. "It's all right," he said, pulling her close. He kissed Joey on the forehead. "Let's all go inside and we'll tell everybody what's been going on since we left this morning."

The barn still smelled of charred wood where part of the west end had burned a few days before. The east end had been converted into living quarters.

Hildy carried Mischief in on her shoulders, looking quickly around the crowded room. "It's so good to be home!" she exclaimed, swinging around. Mischief grabbed the bottom of Hildy's flying brown braids to hang on. "It's not our 'forever' home, but it's better'n that old tent we had by the river!"

She gazed around the room, taking in everything. A water container stood along the left wall with miscellaneous belongings on the floor next to it. Then there was a small kitchen range, a tin cupboard, and a box with a basin of water at the far left corner.

A long expanse of wooden floor led from there to a kitchen cabinet and an old icebox, which was musty and unused. Hildy's father had been able to trade some tools for the double-bed mattress without sheets in the far right-hand corner. He planned to eventually find a bed frame for the mattress. The mattress replaced coats, jackets, and homemade blankets that had first served as bedding after they arrived from their last stop in Illinois.

Against the right-hand wall near the double mattress where her father, stepmother, and baby Joey slept, there was a used dresser for clothes. In front of this was a hand-made kitchen table. Hand-made benches stood on each side for the kids, while two cane-bottom chairs rested at either end of the table. Molly always sat in the chair nearest the wood cook stove, often holding the baby while eating.

Beyond the stove there was a space, then an ancient foot-pedal sewing machine standing in front of a box of clothes. Closer to the right front wall there was another double-bed mattress on the floor. It didn't have any sheets or pillowcases either. All four sisters slept in this bed, alternating head to foot.

In front of that bed was a couch where visitors might sit if there were only two or three. Other belongings were pushed into a right-front corner of the barn-house.

Hildy looked around till she saw Ruby, who was standing silently just inside the front door. Since Joe Corrigan could barely feed his own family, Ruby lived with a neighbor woman named Mrs. Salters, helping with chores in exchange for room and board.

Satisfied with her quick examination of their current dwelling, Hildy turned her attention to the rest of the family. Everyone was talking at once. The pleasant hubbub of her reunited family covered Hildy like a warm blanket.

Little Iola, age three, was trying to tell her daddy about something her ten-year-old practical sister, Elizabeth, had done.

"Daddy," she said in her tiny voice, "'Liz'beth hided food under her pillow again, and Mischief found it and ate it all up last night!"

Joe Corrigan picked up his youngest daughter and gave her a squeeze. "She did, huh?" He turned to Elizabeth, who was named after her mother. "Someday you're going to hide food that'll spoil, and none of us will be able to live in this place."

Hildy caught the hurt look in Elizabeth's eyes and bent down to whisper in her ear. "He's only teasing," she said. "He was away looking for work for so long he doesn't know what it's like to hide a little food in case there isn't any later."

Both older sisters remembered, but they didn't want to tell their father. Elizabeth had started hiding food after her mother died and before their father had married Molly. Joe Corrigan had always tried so hard to find work and feed his family. The girls didn't want him to feel badly because they had sometimes gone hungry.

"Anyway, Elizabeth," Hildy whispered, "Daddy's got a good job now, and Molly's taking good care of us all. You can stop hiding things to eat."

"I know," Elizabeth said, "but it doesn't hurt to save, just in case. Only that raccoon finds everything!"

"Yeah!" five-year-old Sarah added. "He even found some cookies the pastor and his wife brought out from church the other day that 'Lizabeth hid!"

Martha looked up at Hildy. "At first 'Lizabeth blamed us when the cookies disappeared. She tried to get Molly to punish us, but we weren't guilty because that's when we found 'Lizabeth's pile!"

"I remember," Hildy said. "Now all of you go outside and wash your feet. Then I'll listen to your prayers and tell you a story before you sleep. Daddy and Ruby have a lot to talk about with Molly and me, so you all sleep tight, okay?"

After Molly warmed the red beans and homemade biscuits for her husband, Hildy, and Ruby, the younger children were put to bed. The two adults and older cousins sat on upturned lug boxes outside the barn and talked.

Under a star-filled sky, Molly listened to the girls' thoughts about Ozzell Kessick and his nephew, and how Hildy and Mischief had almost been gored by a wild cow, and about the widow Benton and her family.

"So," Hildy said at length, "that's why Ruby's been so quiet since we got here. We know where her father's ranch is, but we don't know where he is. And we've got to find him before the mortgage is foreclosed. Our only lead is in Mariposa County, but we've got no way to get there."

"And ever' day counts," Ruby said softly into the darkness. "We got to work fast, but we don't know whar to start, nohow."

"I do," Molly said quietly. "Let's pray. Then Joe'd better take Ruby to the place where she's staying with those nice folks. Tomorrow we'll start working out plans to get you girls to Mariposa."

The next morning Hildy got up at daybreak, as always. She helped her stepmother prepare breakfast for her father before he left to unload wild cattle in the foothills. Just as the sun rose over the distant rim of the Sierra Nevada Mountains, Hildy took Mischief outside.

A dog barked and Hildy looked up just in time to see a black and tan wire-haired Airedale come bounding up the long dirt lane. "Lindy!" she cried. Then she saw a familiar figure by the Lombardy poplars at the end of the road. "And Spud!"

Spud, fourteen, was strongly built with wide shoulders and a narrow waist. About Hildy's height, he had a handsome, ruddy face with lots of freckles. Even his hands, too big for his body, were covered with freckles. Hildy's heart beat a little faster as she watched her friend, wearing cowboy boots, pants, and a tan work shirt, coming toward her. Instead of the typical crowned hat favored by riders in this cattle country, he sported an aviator-style cap with goggles pushed up on his head. The straps hung loosely below his chin.

"Greetings and felicitations!" Spud called. He smiled and his green eyes lit up in a special way that made Hildy feel funny. Spud loved what Ruby called "two-dollar words."

"Salutations and best wishes yourself," Hildy replied.

Spud grinned broadly. "So, you've been studying my dictionary?" he said. Glancing down at his dog and Hildy's raccoon, he changed the subject. "I see they're getting to know each other a little better."

Although the dog with the docked tail had been taught to ignore the raccoon, Mischief was taking no chances. Dogs were bad news for wild raccoons, and Mischief had been out of the wilds only a few weeks.

She scrambled up Hildy's dress until the girl lifted her up to sit astride her neck. The tiny, sensitive paws gripped Hildy's unbraided hair, which cascaded down to her waist.

Hildy smiled. "I guess Mischief's still not quite sure of Lindy." Feeling the coon's grip on her hair, Hildy suddenly remembered that she hadn't brushed and braided her hair yet. She touched the brown tresses in embarrassment. "I look a fright!" she fussed.

"No, you don't!" Spud said with a grin. "You look like sunshine walking around."

Hildy's face grew warm. Flustered, she tried to change the subject. "If you've come for your dictionary—"

"Keep it a while longer," Spud interrupted. "I came to invite you to see my tree house."

"Tree house?"

"Yep! You know that big tree at the Pattmans' where I've been staying? Well, they let me take some old scrap lumber and fix up a tree house so I wouldn't have to sleep in their barn anymore. It's not a toy house for little kids. It's big enough for a grown person."

"I can hardly wait!" Hildy exclaimed. Then her face clouded. "Oh, but first I'd better tell you about the trip Ruby and I made to the Mother Lode yesterday."

Spud listened carefully and asked questions. Finally he had to leave. "I'll inquire about anyone going to Mariposa," he promised.

After he'd gone whistling down the lane with Lindy, Hildy went inside the barn-house to help Molly and to think.

"There's got to be a way to find Uncle Nate so he can meet

Ruby," she told Molly as they made breakfast for the others. "It seems funny to call him uncle, but that's what he is. He may not even know he has a daughter!"

Molly stirred the pancake batter thoughtfully. "We need to figure out how to save his ranch, too," she said. "And I think it's also our Christian duty to help Mrs. Benton and her family. I can't think how to help with the ranch, but I know how to start helping the Bentons. Mrs. Pattman's coming by this morning to take me shopping. We can stop at the parsonage and tell the pastor about their predicament. He'll tell the others at church, and they'll see that the Bentons at least have something to eat."

Pauline Pattman was the tall, thin, fast-talking neighbor who lived in a chicken coop with her semi-invalid husband. She was the one who had invited the Corrigan family to church right after they moved into the barn-house.

Later that morning, after Mrs. Pattman picked up the family in her pale green Model A Ford, she drove to the Salters and asked permission to take Ruby along. When she explained why, Mrs. Salter readily agreed.

As the packed sedan stopped in front of the town's major grocery store, Molly gasped. "Look at those prices!" she exclaimed.

Hildy silently read the large, hand-lettered signs on the windows advertising specials within: One Pound of Coffee, Thirty Cents. Ten Pounds Granulated Sugar, Fifty-one Cents. Number Two Can of Corn or String Beans, Eight Cents.

Mrs. Pattman read other signs aloud. "Butter, twenty-five and a half cents, solid. Lamb stew, five cents a pound. And steaks—round or sirloin, Grade A—fifteen cents a pound! No wonder a body can't afford to feed a family at such terrible prices!"

Hildy wanted to talk to her cousin about how to get to Mariposa and search for Ruby's father, but so far she hadn't had a chance. As they started into the store's swinging glass door, it opened from the inside.

"Ladies?" A tall, stately man bowed slightly, sweeping his white cowboy hat off his totally white hair. "Come in!" He shifted the bag of groceries he was carrying.

Hildy immediately recognized the eighty-five-year-old gentleman from church. "Oh, hi, Brother Strong," she said. He nodded, running his finger over his large white handlebar mustache with tinges of yellow, and they all exchanged greetings.

Brother Ben Strong never talked about himself, but one of the women at church had told Hildy about the remarkable man.

He had been born in 1849, the year the California Gold Rush started. Then at fifteen, he lied about his age and enlisted in the Confederate Army and was discharged after being wounded. When he was of age, he became a Texas Ranger and later drifted north to Oklahoma Territory, where he served as a U.S. Marshall and became an Indian fighter.

When the Dust Bowl destroyed parts of Oklahoma, Ben Strong came to Lone River. A widower, he was gallant, courtly in manner and speech, and rich from buying and selling land to the county's most successful people—the cattle ranchers.

Hildy looked up at the older gentleman with admiration, then dropped back to whisper to her cousin. "Ruby, if anyone would know how to find your father, Brother Strong would!"

"Yeah!" Ruby's eyes lit up. "He shore would! Let's ask him!"

When the women went into the store to shop, Hildy and Ruby followed the man. His six-foot four-inch body stood tall and straight and his step was quick and firm. He wore highly polished cowboy boots and good quality jeans. As lean as a young willow at the hips, his muscular shoulders made him look much younger than his years.

Hildy and Ruby agreed that his full head of white hair and his square chin made him the most handsome man they'd ever seen. His soft Texas drawl reminded them of Mr. Witt, the Oklahoma rancher who had befriended the girls on their search for Molly and the kids.

Brother Strong led the girls to the curb where he had parked his bright yellow 1929 Packard Victoria with black fenders and brown canvas top. The whitewall balloon tires mounted on bright red wire spokes always looked clean. The matching spare tire in brown covering rested in the well at the base of the right front wheel.

The two headlights mounted between the front fenders and radiator gleamed in the sunlight, and a third, slightly smaller headlamp hung just below the one on the left side. The glistening chrome hood ornament added a final touch of beauty to the classy vehicle.

Brother Ben helped the girls into the backseat of his big Packard and listened attentively while they explained their problem.

"So ye see why we jist got to find my daddy fast, afore it's too late," Ruby concluded. "Ye got any idees?"

"I ought to have," he said in his soft, easy manner. "But I don't right off the top of my head." A look of disappointment crossed Ruby's face, and he added quickly, "I'll study some on it, then get in touch with you."

Opening the car door, he helped the girls down. "You're going to find your father, Ruby," he said firmly. "You have the word of an old gentleman on that."

Hildy was so grateful that she fought back tears. Time was against them. Crying could wait.

CHAPTER SIX

THE COON HUNTER'S THREAT

Hildy's father planned to sleep in the foothills ranch bunk-house instead of coming home that night, so Hildy, her sisters, and Ruby helped Molly prepare for the weekly women's Bible study that had started recently.

Elizabeth, always the practical little sister, offered to sweep the wooden barn floor because it was easy. "See? You just sweep everything through the cracks," she explained.

"Sure," Martha replied, "but all the bugs come through those cracks, too!" There was no money to buy fly spray, so Martha and Sarah drove the swarms of flies out the open door by waving old towels at them. "I'll be glad when we get our 'forever' home that Hildy's always talking about."

"We'll get it," Hildy answered, dusting the table with its cracked oilcloth covering. Mischief, riding in her usual place astride Hildy's neck, made Hildy's task difficult. "I keep looking for it everywhere I go."

"Girls!" Molly exclaimed. "Here they come! Put your things away so everything's neat. Hildy, would you and Ruby please

light the lanterns? You littler ones wash your feet and get ready
for bed."

While the younger sisters protested, Hildy and Ruby stepped
outside, watching the visitors arrive. The women were prompt,
each turning into the long lane just behind the other. One
woman arrived in a buggy behind an old dappled gray farm
horse. The other eleven women came in four old cars. These
represented the few women in the congregation who drove.
Like Molly, most wives depended on their husbands to handle
the cars.

There wasn't enough room inside the barn-house, so the
women brought folding chairs or boxes to sit on while reading
their Bibles outside the sliding barn door. As soon as they arrived, they took pies or cookies inside and set their purses on
the couch, then went around greeting each other.

"Sister Molly!" a stout matron exclaimed, engulfing the host-
ess in a mighty hug. "Thanks for having us."

"I'm glad you could come, Sister Nellie. How's your family?"

Hildy took in the whole scene. Most of the women were
farmwives with round figures, rough hands, and friendly
smiles. Everything about them spoke of hard lives, yet none
complained. With genuine caring, they all inquired about one
another's family, health, and activities.

Hildy lifted Mischief down from her neck and carried her
inside to the couch. "You stay here," she instructed. "I don't
want you getting run over in case any more cars show up. I've
got to help Ruby fill that last lantern and get them all lit."

Outside, while the visitors continued to fellowship in the
gathering dusk, Hildy removed the potato stopper from the
spout on the red kerosene can, and Ruby unscrewed the cap
from the lantern's metal base. Pouring carefully, Hildy filled the
lantern, then replaced the potato and set the can down.

The girls suspended three lanterns from nails on the barn
door and placed two others on upturned lug boxes. Molly told
them they could pass these around and hold them up for anyone
who might have trouble reading.

As the girls placed the last lighted lantern in place, Ruby

started muttering. "What good's all this prayin' and a-studyin' the Bible when my daddy's about to lose his ranch? An' nobody knows where he's even at."

"We'll find him," Hildy assured her. "Since Brother Ben's promised to help, he'll come up with some good ideas. Besides, you're looking at the dark side. Think of the good things the Lord's helped us do."

Ruby didn't hold much with "getting religion" as Hildy had. The blond girl believed in the Lord and the Bible, but God wasn't a real, dependable part of Ruby's life. "Oh, yeah?" she retorted. "Like what?"

Hildy noticed that the wick on one of the lanterns was so high that it was blackening the glass chimney. Hurrying over to it, she turned down the wick. "Well," she said, returning to Ruby's side, "like the way we found Molly after the misunder-standing we had when she took off with the kids and left me behind in the Ozarks."

"What'd the Lord have to do with that?" Ruby asked. "Them thar things jist happened."

"Did they?" Hildy sat down on an upturned bucket as un-seen crickets began singing in the nearby pasture. "How about us meeting Spud when he was hoboing?"

"Spud." The way Ruby said the name, it sounded like a nasty word. At first, she and the boy practically hated each other. They got along a little better now, but they still weren't exactly friends. Molly had told Hildy that was because Ruby and Spud were both independent spirits and were so much alike they refused to see themselves as they really were.

Hildy tried once more to convince Ruby that the Lord had been helping them. "How do you explain lightning striking my horse in Oklahoma and knocking the shoes off, when I didn't feel a thing?"

Ruby shrugged. "Jist lucky, I guess."

"You don't see how the Lord is working?"

"Maybe it works fer ye, but I ain't never knowed nothin' in life but meanness and misery." Ruby scuffed her bare foot in the dirt. "What kinda God is that fer a body to believe in?"

"He's going to help us find your father, Ruby—the father you've never seen, the one that may not even know you exist."

"I still don't see it," Ruby said. She walked off down the long driveway toward the Lombardy poplars.

Although Hildy ached for her cousin, she knew there was nothing more she could do or say. She went inside the barn-house where Molly was listening to the smaller girls say their prayers.

Reaching into a lug box, Hildy picked up her small, black, well-worn Bible. Her Grandpa Corrigan had given it to her the month before in Illinois. It had belonged to his father.

Four generations have read this Bible, Hildy thought. She looked over at Mischief, who was sitting on the back of the couch, and gave her a pat. As she walked out into the lantern light again, she corrected herself. *Well, I guess we can't count Daddy because he's like Ruby. He has a hard time believing, too.* For a moment, Hildy wondered why, then dismissed the question to join the women.

Before starting the actual Bible study, the ladies always discussed one another's needs and those of the community. That night Molly told about Mrs. Benton, and Hildy added some details. The other women decided to collect food and clothes for the family. When Hildy told them about Ruby's predicament, the church women wanted to pray for Ruby to find her father, but that raised some hard questions in Hildy's mind.

What if Nate Konning was found in time to pay off the mortgage but he didn't have the money? And who actually held the mortgage? Would that person give an extension or demand payment in full on time?

Hildy had an uneasy feeling that she knew who held the mortgage. She could check that out if she could get a ride back to the Monitor County Courthouse at Hardrock. But it was more important to find Ruby's father fast.

As the night wore on, the women prayed for each of their families, for healing of sick and hurt bodies, for daily food and shelter, and for continued strength to survive the Depression. There was a strange bond among them. They all lived in hard circumstances, yet their faith in God helped them keep going.

Hildy wished Ruby had stayed for the prayer time, but she was somewhere out in the darkness, alone with her thoughts.

The Bible study followed prayer, and then at about nine-thirty the session ended. It was customary for the women to then file inside to get their dessert and go back outdoors to eat and visit.

Hildy led the way into the barn-house. In the dim light of the lamp burning low on the kitchen table, she saw that her sisters and baby brother were sleeping. But Mischief sat up wide awake, her eyes glowing a strange pale blue-green.

"Oh no, Mischief!" Hildy scolded. "What've you done?"

"Our purses!" the stout farm woman cried. "That coon has opened every one and mixed everything together!"

As usual when her forepaws were busy, Mischief stared off into the distance. Her sensitive, agile "fingers" continued exploring the contents of a dozen purses without any concern for the sudden, agitated appearance of a dozen good church women.

Each of their purses had been opened and emptied. Although the women didn't wear cosmetics or jewelry, their handkerchiefs, coins, glass cases, keys, personal identification, mirrors, and combs were scattered all over the couch and on the wooden barn floor.

"Oh, my!" Molly whispered as she hastily lifted the raccoon out of the disaster. "Oh, my!" Each exclamation sounded more and more distressed. "Oh, my!"

Some of the visiting women reacted with indignation. "What a terrible mess! We'll never get this stuff separated!"

Others tried to view the situation with humor. "You've got to admit that little rascal did a thorough job of mixing everything up!"

Hildy and her stepmother were very embarrassed. After sorting and reclaiming items, the visitors departed with their belongings, and Molly mumbled something about never being able to live down the humiliation. Molly didn't blame Mischief, but she did tell Hildy she would have to be more responsible with her pet.

When Ruby returned from her solitary walk, Molly made arrangements for her to stay the night. As the two girls got ready for bed, Hildy told Ruby what Mischief had done. "Bet this is one Bible study those women will never forget!" Hildy said, laughing.

In spite of her lack of sleep, Hildy got up the next morning at dawn. Mischief was a nocturnal animal by nature, so Hildy was used to the coon roaming around outside at night. Usually the animal waited in the adjacent open part of the barn for Hildy to get up. But that morning the little masked animal wasn't there, so Hildy went looking for her.

After a quick check in the outhouse, tank house, and other possible hiding places, Hildy started down the long lane, calling for Mischief. She also hoped Spud might come whistling down the lane with news about a ride to Mariposa.

But as Hildy surveyed the area, she saw nothing except the Lombardy poplars standing silently by the country road. Hildy began to panic. "Where could Mischief be? I hope she's okay!"

Hildy stood in the driveway, her eyes darting everywhere for a sign of Mischief. Then as she turned back toward the barn-house, she heard Spud's familiar happy whistle. Instantly, Hildy felt better.

Spud cut across the adjacent Ladino clover field, and Hildy noticed he had replaced his usual aviator's cap with a wide-brimmed cowboy hat. *He must expect to be out in the hot sun today*, she thought.

"Guess what?" he called, lifting the lower strand of barbed wire so Lindy could pass under. Without waiting for an answer, Spud continued. "I have secured a ride for us to Mariposa!"

Hildy's face lit up, and she ran to the fence. She absently patted the dog's head while Spud climbed between the second and third strands of wire. "You have?"

"Mr. Zummer—neighbor—is motoring there on business to-day. We can ride along if we're ready by seven o'clock this morn-ing. He wants to drive while it's cool."

Hildy's emotions churned with a mixture of happiness and concern. "Oh, that's wonderful! But that's less than an hour, and I can't find Mischief."

"You go get dressed. Lindy and I'll find her."

Hildy ran to the barn-house and slipped into her dress as she told Ruby the good news. Ruby quickly pulled on her overalls and the two girls grabbed a couple of cold biscuits as they ran out the barn door. Just then Spud approached with Mischief in his arms.

Hildy ran up and took the little raccoon. "Where'd you find her?"

"Over there on an old stump in that big blackberry patch. I didn't actually find her. Lindy's proboscis did," he said, grinning down as the Airedale continued to sniff. Then he looked at Hildy with concern. "Uh . . . she's been hurt."

"She has?" Hildy carefully examined her pet. "That looks like a bite wound!"

"How do you suppose that happened?" Ruby asked.

"Dog, most likely," Spud replied. "I heard hounds baying last night. Up in my tree house I had a pretty good view, but I couldn't see anything."

"You mean . . . you think a hound caught her?"

"Maybe nipped her because there's only that one puncture. Coons are smart, so she got away, but . . ."

Bright sunlight reflected off a windshield, and his sentence trailed off incomplete, as a car turned off the county road into the long lane.

"Who's that coming here so early?" Hildy asked, preoccupied with what she could use to cleanse Mischief's wounds.

"Our ride to Mariposa, I guess," Spud answered. "But that looks like an old Star that's had the back cut off to make a pickup. I don't think that's Mr. Zummer's."

"I kin see hounds in the back end," Ruby said.

Mischief scrambled up onto Hildy's neck as the coon got the hounds' scent.

A man as thin as a pencil stopped the automobile and got out. Dusting off his dirty overalls, he shouted at the two hounds. They tucked their tails and quit barking.

A boy about fifteen, dressed in tattered overalls and a grimy cap, slid out of the passenger's side and walked over beside his father. "There it is, Pa!" He pointed at Mischief. "I told ye Ol' Blue got hisself in a fight with a coon! See the blood on that one? That's the coon that done it!"

The thin man approached, kicking up dust with his heavy work shoes. "Howdy," he said, nodding to Hildy and then Spud. "Reckon muh boy was right about hearin' y'all had a coon. I come to swap for it."

Hildy shook her head. "I couldn't trade Mischief off!"

The boy stomped his foot. "Make her do it, Pa!" he hollered.

The man reached into the bib pocket of his overalls and produced a pouch of loose chewing tobacco. "Make ye a right smart deal," he said, waving the tobacco at the coon before stuffing the chew in his mouth.

Spud took a step forward. "You heard Hildy," he said evenly. "No deal."

The man turned cold, hard eyes on Spud. "You own that coon, boy?"

"No, she does! And don't call me boy!"

"Yeah, who d'ye think ye air, anyway?" Ruby shouted angrily.

"If'n ye don't own it, then I'd be obliged if y'all keep outta this," the man retorted. "Now, Hildy, if'n that's yore name, I ain't got no cash money, but I'll make ye a pow'rful good swap. Give ye a choice of sweet corn, fresh aigs, some pullets, a gunny sack of 'taters er a lug box of freestone peaches. Maybe throw in somethin' to boot."

Ruby started to argue, but Spud quietly reached out and took both girls by the shoulder. "Go back in the house," he said softly.

Hildy opened her mouth to protest but yielded to Spud's persistent pressure on her shoulder. With Mischief hanging on to her hair, Hildy turned away.

"Now ye done it!" the man cried. "I tried to be nice, but ye wouldn't let me. Y'all win this time, but we'll be back. And if'n ye won't swap, then me'n muh boy will see that coon dead!"

CHAPTER
SEVEN

THE CLUE

The long drive to Mariposa took Hildy, Ruby, and Spud down the San Joaquin Valley and then east into the hot, dry foothills heading toward Yosemite. Hildy didn't join in the conversation. Withdrawn and deep in thought, she didn't even glance at houses that might fit her mental picture of what a "forever" home should look like.

Who was that man and boy who threatened Mischief's life? she wondered. *Did I treat Mischief's wound properly?* Mr. Zummer came so quickly after the other man left that there was barely enough time to take care of the raccoon and get permission from her stepmother to make the trip. She couldn't help but wonder if they really would find Ruby's father that day.

Mr. Zummer, a heavy-set man with a red face, stopped at a turkey ranch outside Mariposa to ask directions to the nearest cattle ranch.

Ruby wrinkled her nose at the stench. "What's that thar I'm a-smellin'?" she asked.

"Those are the brooder houses," Spud told her.

The incessant gobbling of thousands of bronze birds filled the air as Mr. Zummer stopped beside the small frame house under a sycamore tree.

Before anybody could get out of the car, a bald man of medium build stepped out of the screened-in back porch. He shoved the twin muzzles of a double-barreled shotgun through a hole in the rusted screen. "State your business!" he called.

Hildy blinked and looked at Spud and Ruby in surprise.

Ruby leaned closer to her cousin. "What d'ye reckon's wrong with him?" she whispered.

Spud stuck his head out the window. "We're looking for a man named Nate Konning!" he shouted. "You know him?"

The man in the porch shadows didn't answer for a moment. Then he withdrew the shotgun barrel and pushed open the squeaky screen door. He stood on the back step with the gun under his right arm. "What d'you want to know?" he demanded.

Hildy twisted her fingers nervously. "He's my uncle," she called back. "We've got to find him."

The man leaned forward, studying the car's occupants. "You're just kids—'ceptin' the driver," he said with apparent relief.

Ruby opened the right rear door and stepped out. "He's my pa. We heerd he might be a-workin' 'round here."

The man broke the shotgun and ejected the red shells. "Sorry, kids. Last night my foreman surprised some men trying to steal turkeys. One of them took a shot at him, so I'm a little skittish."

The young people nodded in understanding.

"I can understand a man maybe trying to steal to feed his family, but when somebody shoots a gun, I get plumb agitated," the man explained. "Now, gimme the name again of this feller you're looking for."

When the man had the full story, he shrugged. "I know practically everybody around these parts, but nobody by that name. However, if he's a rider, there's only one rancher around here who's hired anybody since this Depression started. Name's Lane—Bob Lane. I'll give you directions to his place."

Mr. Zummer drove the kids to the Lane Ranch, sprawled on gently rolling hills and set back in a grove of cottonwood trees by a slow-moving creek. Bob Lane was a big man, whose stomach rolled well over his large belt buckle. He listened attentively as the kids told him why they had come.

"Nate Konning, you say?" he asked in a gravelly voice.

"Or Slim or Highpockets—nicknames like that," Hildy added hopefully.

"A lot of men drift through here, looking for work as riders. So it's possible he was one of them. But I just can't help you. Sorry, kids."

Since Mr. Zummer had to drive into town on business, the kids asked everyone they met there if anyone had seen a tall, slender rider. Nobody was helpful.

Finally, late in the afternoon, they headed back toward Lone River.

Ruby sat with Hildy in the backseat, staring out the window until finally she exploded. "Not one blesset thing to go on!" she cried. "They's no place to turn—nary a lead left!"

Hildy patted her hand. "Don't get discouraged," she comforted. "We've still got time."

"Ye got time," she argued angrily, "but I don't. It's not like ye a-lookin' fer yore 'forever' home. It's my *daddy* we're a-talkin' 'bout! It hurts so bad to finally find out I got me a real one, only I cain't find him no more now than when I wasn't even shore I had one!"

Hildy remembered the awful pain she had felt when she was separated from her family. Only this was worse for Ruby. She had never had a real family. "Tomorrow's Sunday," she said hopefully. "I'll ask the pastor to pray for—"

"That don't do no good!" Ruby interrupted. "Leastwise, not fer me."

Hildy looked thoughtfully at her cousin, wondering if she had been privately praying in the past. But it was obvious that Ruby didn't want to talk about it, so Hildy changed the subject. All the way home, however, she prayed silently for all the things that were bothering her.

Spud wouldn't go to church with Hildy, either. He had gone once, right after arriving in Lone River, but after that, he had politely refused without giving any reasons. Hildy assumed it had something to do with his running away from his strict father. Still, sometimes Hildy would find him sitting on the bottom step in front of the church, waiting for her.

When the Corrigan kids first started going to church, Pastor Hyde picked them up in his small house trailer. Lately, though, Brother Clive, an elderly widower, had volunteered to bring Hildy, Molly, and the other five Corrigan children with him in his old Dodge sedan.

They all wore shoes because each had one pair worn only on Sunday. Joe and Molly had bought a second pair of shoes for each child the year before when school started, but these were all worn out or outgrown. Except for church, everyone would go barefooted until school started.

As their neighbor Brother Clive parked his Dodge on the side street by the long, white church with the tall bell tower, Hildy saw Ben Strong getting out of his Packard.

She ran up to him. "Any ideas to help find Ruby's father?" she asked.

He flicked his yellowish-white handlebar mustache with the back of his forefinger. "Some," he admitted. "Meet me after church and I'll fill you in. I'm an usher today, so I can't say more right now."

Hildy felt restless during the service. And when the pastor announced that he was going to preach on the Prodigal Son, she moaned to herself. *I've heard dozens of sermons about that*, she thought. *I don't want to hear another.*

She tuned out the sermon, and her eyes probed the stained glass windows. They actually were made of multi-colored paper pasted to the clear windowpane. Hildy's attention wandered to the altar in front of the pulpit, past the dozen-voice choir to a poster near the door of the pastor's office.

The poster was a color print of the world as a globe with countless hands of all colors holding it up. The words underneath proclaimed: It Isn't Heavy If We All Help.

At that moment, Hildy didn't care about the world. *We've got to find Ruby's father!* she told herself. *And fast! But how?*

Brother Hyde's rising voice interrupted Hildy's thoughts. ". . . so this Jewish man, whose religion prohibited him from even eating pork, was reduced to feeding hogs!" he exclaimed. "That'd be something like you cattlemen having to become sheepherders."

"Amen!" a small stockman shouted from what was called "The Amen Corner." The small section was down front in the center of the church, not quite in front of the pastor, but slightly to the left end of the second row of pews. Half a dozen of the church's most staunch supporters, mostly dirt farmers and their wives, sat there. Periodically, one good brother would exclaim aloud, "That's so, Brother!" or "Amen" to support what the preacher had just said.

Hildy smiled at the idea of a cowboy herding sheep. Her father was a cowboy, but he hated sheep. He had often said that, unlike cows, they ate the grass too close to the ground. Sheep even pulled up the roots. And their sharp hooves reduced the soil to dust. But worst of all, sheep smelled bad.

Dad'd never be a sheepherder, Hildy told herself with satisfaction. Her mind wandered again, remembering how he traveled from state to state looking for work. He had often worked two jobs to support his family. He had picked cotton, been an oil-field roughneck, worked as a machinist, and labored on the railroad. *But I can't imagine him getting down off his cutting horse to herd smelly sheep*, she thought.

Suddenly she remembered the sheepherder she had helped get away from Rob Kessick and his friends. *He wore cowboy boots*, she thought. *I wonder why. And why did Ozzell Kessick mislead Ruby and me about where her father might be?*

During the congregational prayer, when everyone knelt in the pews, the pastor prayed about Ruby and her father. He only mentioned them briefly because the times were hard and many hurting people in the congregation had urgent prayer requests.

Hildy sighed, wondering if God heard such short prayers. Then she remembered that some of her own most effective prayers had been very short but from the heart.

After church, Hildy hurried past the old folks wearing suits that smelled of mothballs and dresses that were long out of style. Her heart was so filled with concern for Ruby that she didn't feel like shaking calloused hands and making small talk. She wanted to escape outdoors.

At the top of the high, concrete steps, she stopped and looked down. Spud sat on the bottom step alone, wearing his cowboy boots, jeans, and shirt with his favorite aviator's cap.

"Spud!" she exclaimed, hurrying down the steps toward him. "Why didn't you come inside where it's comfortable?"

Standing, he looked at her with those green eyes that made Hildy feel funny. "I don't mind waiting," he said. "I had nothing else to do."

"Well, you do now!" Hildy cried, almost skipping down the stairs. "I want you to meet the old Texas Ranger who's going to help us find Ruby's father."

When Ben Strong came down the stairs, Hildy led Spud over to him. "Brother Ben," she said to the stately old gentleman with a white cowboy hat in his hand, "I want you to meet a friend. This is Spud. He hates his real name. But he's going to help us find Ruby's father."

"Howdy, Spud," the old ranger said, shaking the boy's hand warmly. "I like your cap."

Spud snatched his aviator-style cap off. "It's in honor of Lindbergh," he explained. "This is just like the one he wore while flying the Atlantic."

"You have the look of eagles in your eyes, too, Spud," the old man said, "if I'm any judge of men."

Hildy looked at Spud, startled. She'd never thought of his strange green eyes that way, but it seemed to fit.

Obviously, Spud had never thought of his eyes like that, either. "Uh . . . thanks," he said awkwardly.

A warm glow swept over Hildy. *They like each other*, she thought. *Two of the nicest people I know really like each other*.

The white-haired man set his Stetson back on his head and thoughtfully stroked his handlebar mustache. "So you're going to help, are you, Spud?"

"Yessir! Any way I can."

"Then Hildy won't mind if you listen while I make a suggestion about where to start?"

"Of course not," Hildy agreed.

Brother Ben led the way to the shade of a sycamore tree planted between the curb and sidewalk. "I think," he said softly, his drawl becoming more pronounced than usual, "we should start by looking at the Monitor County records. Let's see who holds the mortgage on the ranch Ruby's father owns."

Hildy leaned forward. "I have a hunch who that is," she told them. "But how will that help us find Uncle Nate?"

"Might give us a motive, for one thing," the old gentleman replied. "And, like you, Hildy, I have an idea who holds the mortgage."

Spud's eyes widened. "You both have an idea of who it is, so . . . who is it?"

Hildy took a deep breath. "Ozzell Kessick," she answered.

The old man smiled. "Hildy, you'd have made a mighty good ranger."

Spud frowned. "You mean the cattleman whose nephew gave Hildy and Ruby a hard time at Simple Justice?"

"The same," the old man replied. "Now, if you'll make arrangements with Ruby, we'll all drive up there tomorrow and start our investigation. I think we're about to learn some things that could very well lead us to Ruby's father."

CHAPTER EIGHT

DISTANT SMOKE

When their neighbor Brother Clive slowed his loaded Dodge sedan at the Corrigans' driveway, Hildy was fairly bursting to tell Ruby about their upcoming trip with the old ranger. But the moment the sedan turned into the dirt road, Hildy's heart jumped.

"Molly! Look!" Hildy pointed toward an old Star coupe modified with a homemade wooden back to make a pickup. It was parked in front of the barn-house. "It's them again!"

"Who?" Her stepmother shifted baby Joey on her lap and turned around in the front seat to look back at Hildy. "I don't recognize—"

"The man who wanted to trade for Mischief. Oh, I hope they haven't done anything to Ruby!"

The moment the Dodge stopped, Hildy leaped out onto the running board. In her tight-fitting Sunday shoes, she sprinted through the dust toward the pickup. The man and his son stared at her through the windshield, but the dogs were gone from the back.

"Ruby!" Hildy hollered. "Where's Mischief?"

The skinny man slid out from under the steering wheel while

his son jumped down from the passenger side.

The man shifted a wad of chewing tobacco to his other cheek. "If ye mean that blond gal, she's a-settin' inside the barn with a pitchfork in one hand and that fool coon in t'other," he said.

Hildy's stepmother hurried over with the baby in her arms.

"Missus," the man said, "if that there's yore gal in there, I'd be plumb obliged if'n ye told her to turn over that coon peaceable like."

"Yeah!" the boy said with a sneer. "So we kin sic our hounds loose on it!"

"My stars!" Molly exclaimed. "Whatever are you talking about?"

Suddenly the heavy barn door slid open just enough for Ruby to squeeze through. Everyone looked up. Ruby held a pitchfork in both hands while the raccoon rode on her neck. Mischief's left hind foot hooked into Ruby's overall bib while she braced her right foot against the girl's shoulder. Both tiny front paws gripped Ruby's short blond hair.

"Now that things air a leetle more even," Ruby said through clenched teeth, "we'll see who's a-goin' to keep this here coon!"

"Ruby!" Molly scolded sharply. "Put that pitchfork down before you hurt somebody!"

"That's egg-zackly what I'm a-aimin' to do with it, Molly," Ruby announced. She advanced steadily, the pitchfork pointed straight at the man and boy.

"Ruby!" Hildy ran to her cousin and shoved the tines down. "Get hold of yourself!"

Ruby seethed in anger. "They done started it! Ask 'em!"

The thin man sprayed an ugly stream of tobacco juice into the dust. "That ain't the pure truth of it, missuz," he said, looking back at Molly. "That there coon caught my best cold-nose pappy hound alone, walkin' 'long beside our wooden fence—"

"Mindin' his own business," the boy broke in. "Wasn't hurtin' nobody when yore o'nry coon done dropped down on him in a sneaky attack. Like to cut Ol' Blue's ears to ribbons afore he could git away and run home to us."

" 'Tain't nothin' but lies!" Ruby shouted. "Mischief was here with me the whole blesset mornin'. Maybe it was a cat caught yore dawg. I heerd tell of a big ol' mean tomcat that's done that same thing to dogs hereabouts. Maybe he done it. Mischief shore didn't!" She waved the pitchfork in the air again. "Now, Molly, make them two get offa the prop'ity afore I fergit myself and teach 'em some manners!"

Hildy wanted to smile, but she knew the charges against her pet were serious, though untrue. Reaching up, she took the little masked animal from Ruby's neck and settled it on her own. Mischief made low guttural sounds at the two visitors.

Molly turned to the stranger. "Mister . . ."

"Jarman, ma'am. Charley Jarman," the man introduced himself. "This here's muh boy, Rafe. We live down yonder." He pointed across the clover field to the west.

"Mr. Jarman—and Rafe," Molly continued, "I believe Ruby. Now I'm inviting you two to get off this property before I have the law on you."

Hildy wanted to cheer. It was the first time since Molly had come into the family that she had an opportunity to defend her brood. Hildy had taken over that responsibility when her mother died, but it wasn't something a twelve-year-old wanted too much.

"Ma'am," the coon hunter said with quiet deadliness, "y'all shouldn't have said that. I was willin' before to overlook yore daughter's remarks when she wouldn't listen to reason. But now that you done sided with these gals, I'm plumb obliged to get rid of that mean coon as fast as me'n muh boy kin do it!"

When the Jarmans were gone, Hildy and her family discussed how they could protect Mischief.

Hildy scratched her head. "We just can't keep her penned up all the time," she said. "She's not a dog we can train not to go running around the neighborhood at night."

Molly nodded. "Mischief feeds herself 'cause we can't afford any extra mouths. She's got to stay free. So sooner or later, the Jarmans will poison her, or trap her, or shoot—"

"No-o-o!" Elizabeth screamed, jumping up from the bench by the table. "Hildy, you've got to keep Mischief with you all the time!"

"I can't do that!" Hildy objected. "Like when Brother Ben takes Ruby, Spud, and me up to see who holds the mortgage—"

"What?" Ruby cried, jumping over to grab her cousin by the shoulders. "We're a-goin'?"

"We're going. Tomorrow!"

"Why didn't ye tell me?"

"Guess I forgot in all the excitement with the Jarmans," Hildy explained. "Let's go inside and I'll tell you everything—including who the old ranger and I think holds the mortgage on your father's ranch."

"Ha!" Ruby laughed. "I'll tell ye who. Ozzie Kessick, that's who. I done figured that out already. I jist don't know why."

Lunch dishes were washed, dried, and put away before every aspect of the case had been discussed. About three o'clock as Hildy's hands worked a big batch of dough, making buns for supper, she heard Spud come whistling down the lane. Flour covered the girl's arms to the elbow and part of her face.

"Don't let him in!" she whispered fiercely. "Keep him outside until I get cleaned up."

"Why?" Elizabeth asked. "Don't you think a boyfriend should see his girl being domestic?"

"He's not my boyfriend," Hildy protested. "Molly, please help me!"

While her stepmother herded the other girls outside, Hildy turned to the washbasin in the back corner of the living quarters. "Oh, why can't we have a telephone or something so people would have to call first instead of just dropping by unexpectedly?"

After she had made hasty repairs to her clothing and hair, Hildy walked outside. Her little sisters ran giggling past her into the barn-house.

Elizabeth stopped momentarily. "They're at it again!" she blurted.

"Who?"

"Ruby and Spud!"

Hildy ran. Ruby and Spud were arguing again, and Molly was unsuccessfully trying to calm them down.

Ruby's face flushed. "I shoulda whupped ye good the fust time I ever laid eyes on ye back in the Ozarks!"

Spud sputtered, "If you weren't a girl, I'd—"

"Ruby! Spud!" Hildy shouted. "Stop it. You can't ride up to the mountains together if you're going to act like that."

Ruby's temper flared. "He called me a vi-too-per . . . uh . . ."

"Vituperative," Spud said. "Vituperative vixen!"

"He knows I don't know what it means, but I know it's somethin' low down and o'nry!" Ruby fussed.

Molly took charge. "Let's have no more of this," she said, separating the two.

The angry flush faded from Ruby's face, and she lowered her voice. "I got to see them courthouse papers," she said. "Then I got to find my daddy afore he loses that thar place. But I don't need Spud's help!"

"Yes, you do," Hildy argued. "Please, both of you!"

Spud's body relaxed. "I want to help, Ruby. Really, I do."

"There," Hildy said with satisfaction. "That's better. Now let's talk about what we're going to do tomorrow—especially what we should do with Mischief while we're gone."

Ruby and Spud slowly got over their tiff and helped with Hildy's discussions. However, they couldn't decide the best way to protect Mischief. That was another worry for Hildy.

The next morning when the old ranger arrived in his big yellow Packard, he listened to Hildy's problem. "That's easy," he said, flipping his mustache. "Bring Mischief along. But you probably can't take the animal into the courthouse."

Spud, who wore his wide-brimmed hat as protection against the sun, shoved the brim back. "I'll stay outside with her," he offered.

In twenty minutes or so, the Packard left the flat valley behind and began climbing into the first little foothills of the great Sierra Nevada Mountains.

Hildy first felt some concern about how good a driver an eighty-five-year-old man could be. But he proved himself competent and cautious, especially on curves where there were no guard rails. He sounded the horn before starting around each turn. Hildy relaxed.

For some time, everyone freely shared ideas of what they would find at the courthouse, and what they could do to locate Nate Konning. As the car climbed higher, a gradual silence settled over the group.

Hildy glanced at her cousin. Ruby had leaned her head back and dozed off. Mischief lay asleep between the girls.

Hildy bent forward against the back of the front seat to talk to Spud. "Did you ever hear from your family?" she asked.

He turned toward her. "Not since you talked me into writing them. I told you my old man wouldn't write! That reprobate probably wouldn't let my mother or sisters write either."

There was a hardness in Spud's voice that almost frightened Hildy. She didn't like the disrespectful way he spoke of his father, either, but she knew it didn't do any good to talk to him about it.

"You could write again," she suggested.

"Ha!" His tone was so sharp that Ruby jumped.

"Please?" Hildy said softly. "Even if they don't answer, I'm sure your mother will want to know you're well."

Ruby leaned forward. "Hildy, why don't ye jist leave a body be? Y'all couldn't git me to write and make up with my grandma. So why should ye waste yore time a-tellin' Spud to write his kin?"

Hildy sighed. How could she explain to anyone how important family was to her. "I wrote my granny," she said.

"An' she never answered ye, neither," Ruby retorted. "Anyway, yore granny's so mean that yore better off without her. Same with me and her mean sister."

Hildy looked at the old ranger but he said nothing. She felt embarrassed about the personal discussion in front of such a distinguished, self-assured man. "Someday," she said, "I'm going back to make up with Granny."

"An' I'm a-goin' back, too," Ruby promised. "But only when I kin show off my daddy to all them people who said such turrible things about me all my life. We'll show 'em, my daddy and me!"

Spud rubbed his hand over his face thoughtfully. "If my old man and I ever reconcile, Hildy, maybe I'd go back to New York and never see you again."

The thought came like a punch in the stomach to Hildy. She sank back into the seat with a strange, sad feeling inside, and they made the rest of the trip in silence.

At the county courthouse, Spud stayed with Mischief in the car while the girls and Brother Strong went inside.

After a few minutes of searching the public records, Hildy looked up excitedly. "We were right!" she exclaimed. "The mortgage is held by Ozzell Kessick."

They thanked the clerk and started walking down the echoing old hallway toward the outside door.

"I knowed it," Ruby moaned. "I knowed it. An' now I know why. That thar Kessick wants my daddy's ranch. But why? It ain't big enough to run many head of cattle on."

The old ranger flipped his mustache. "I've been analyzing what you've all told me, and I have a theory. But I'd rather not say until I've seen the ranch. Let's drive out and see if I'm right."

As the big Packard eased along the dusty road beneath the frowning mass of Thunder Mountain, Brother Strong glanced back at the girls. "I hope Mrs. Benton won't be offended, but I put some groceries and clothes in the trunk for her and the kids," he said.

"That's pow'rful nice of ye," Ruby said. "She's a nice widder woman that the world's done kicked in the teeth harder'n anybody should be."

Suddenly Hildy leaned forward and pointed through the windshield. "Smoke!" she cried.

"Lots of it!" Spud agreed. "Not light-colored like grass. It's black, more like—"

"It looks like when Hildy's barn-house was set a-fahr," Ruby said. "I betcha them night riders done what they threatened. They're a-burnin' my daddy's place up! And the widder and kids air thar!"

Chapter Nine

THE NIGHT RIDERS STRIKE

The big Packard roared down the treeless lane toward the sod house where the widow Benton lived with her children. Not seeing the children outside, Hildy's eyes flickered anxiously to the barn. A small crowd of people in cars, on bicycles, or horseback had come to watch the fire.

"There!" Hildy exclaimed, pointing toward what was left of the barn. "Mrs. Benton and all the kids are there. They're safe!"

"The barn shore ain't," Ruby cried.

Hildy shook her head. The barn lay in total ruins. The rural fire department's Liberty pumper spewed the last of its water tank onto the collapsed, blackened timbers, and volunteer fire fighters prepared to return to the station.

The oldest Benton boy seemed to recognize Hildy and her friends and raced barefoot toward them. His barefoot mother and siblings hurried after him.

Jacob leaped upon the Packard's left running board and thrust his face into the car between the front and back seats.

Frightened, excited words tumbled from his smudged,

smoke-streaked face. "Them night riders done it, jist like they said they would! Only this time they come jist at daybreak—two of 'em. Had han'kerchiefs over their faces. Cut the barb' wahr and drove a herd o' cattle through. Maybe twenty head. Then they set the barn a-fahr!"

Hildy hadn't noticed the tangle of barbed wire. It had been cut in the middle, curling both ends back, and dragged off to the side so horses and cattle could move through without getting cut by the nasty barbs.

"Everybody all right?" Hildy asked.

The boy nodded, his eyes still wide with excitement. "Jist scared, I reckon. Here comes Ma. She'll tell ye what happened."

Out of breath and trailed by the rest of her dirty-faced kids, the widow approached the driver's side of the car. "Howdy, folks! Reckon the excitement's 'bout over, so yore welcome to light and sit a spell!"

As they all got out, Hildy began the introductions. "This is Brother Ben Strong from our church, Mrs. Benton."

"Pleased to meetcha," the widow said, bobbing her head. Her uncombed brunette hair looked grimy, and her glasses were smudged with smoke and ashes.

The old ranger gallantly removed his big white cowboy hat, bowed slightly and said, "Ma'am."

Jacob looked around. "Reckon they's no shade hereabouts now that the barn's gone. We'll have to stand in the sun."

Hildy quickly realized that was true. The dugout was too close to the earth to cast much shadow, and there wasn't a single tree, bush, or building in the hot, barren stretch of gently rolling hills. The hills stretched toward the horizon in every direction except east. There Thunder Mountain's black, massive bulk stood solidly under the boiling sun.

The old ranger set his Stetson back on his head. "I ort to look around before the firemen leave," he said. "The rest of y'all might find a little shade by hunkerin' down beside the car."

Hildy protested. "I want to go with you, Brother Ben—I mean, as long as everyone's all right."

Ruby and Spud agreed, and Hildy turned back to the car to

lift Mischief out. The coon struggled and fled back to the safety of the back floorboards.

"She's afraid of the smoke's smell," Hildy explained.

"Kin we play with him?" the two oldest girls asked together.

"Mischief's a *her*," Hildy corrected, "and she's so upset she might not let you get close."

The widow walked over to the raccoon and smiled slightly. "I'd be obliged if y'all'd let my young'uns try," she said. "We got no pet, no animals, no radio, no near neighbors—not even no newspapers or dime novels. The kids'd be mighty gentle with yore coon."

Hildy sighed when she saw the pleading in the Benton children's eyes. "All right," she gave in. "Sit in the car's shade and take turns petting Mischief."

All except the baby crowded around with glad cries. Mischief seemed to sense the love in the strokes of the tiny, dirty hands. The raccoon rolled over so they could pet the soft fur on her underside.

Taking her youngest daughter with her, Mrs. Benton led the way back to the smoking ruins. Hildy, Ruby, Spud, and Brother Strong followed.

As they neared the barn, the volunteer fire chief met them. Since he was wearing an oil-smeared cap and mechanic's coveralls and smelled of grease, Hildy guessed he had probably been repairing a car when the barn fire report came in.

The chief took off his oily cap. "It was too far gone to save it when we got here, ma'am," he said. "I'm mighty sorry." He pulled a grimy notebook and stub of a pencil from his coverall pockets. "I got to ask some questions."

Ben Strong's ears perked up. "Mind if we listen?" he asked.

"Listen if you want," the fire chief replied.

Everyone crowded around while the widow explained that she and her family were squatting on the unoccupied ranch. She didn't know where the owner was.

"It wasn't more'n first light when I heerd them cattle a-comin' down the lane," she continued. "I looked out and seed they was wild with turrible horns! I was skeered they'd hurt my young'uns, so we hid in the house while them masked riders cut the wahr an' drove the stock through. One kept the stock a-movin' while the other man tetched off the barn with a leetle can o' kerosene and some gofer matches."

Hildy had heard her father talk about the new gofer matches. There were a number of them in a little book. One match was removed, the cover closed, then the match struck against a strip of abrasive paper on the cover. Joe Corrigan had said that the matches got their name "because when you light one, it goes right out, so you gofer another."

The chief made notes as Mrs. Benton talked. "Just a couple more questions, ma'am," he said. "Any idea who those riders were?"

"We couldn't tell because they had pulled their neckerchiefs up over their faces."

"Any brands on horses or cows?" the chief asked.

"Didn't notice any."

Closing his notebook, the fire chief stuck it and the pencil stub into his coverall pocket. "I'll turn in a report to the sheriff," he promised. "A deputy'll be around to follow up on things."

As he turned back to his volunteers, Ruby moaned, "Why'd they do this to my daddy?" she asked. "If'n he was here, I bet they'd a-never done nothin' like that!"

Ben Strong stood looking at the cut in the volcanic mountain through which the masked riders had driven the cattle. "I suspected the reason Kessick wanted this place," he said quietly.

"Why, Brother Ben?" Ruby asked.

The old ranger pointed to the forty-foot-wide opening in Thunder Mountain. "Before we drove up here, I did some research. That pass is the only one in this whole mountain. It's nearly twenty miles around either end. For years, cattlemen drove their stock through here, looking for better pasture. Then Nate Konning filed claim to this open land, built that dugout and the barn, and fenced off The Pass."

Spud's eyes lit up. "With this natural pass closed, stockmen like Kessick had to drive their cattle around either end," he said. "That must cost time and money."

Ben Strong nodded. "Ten miles a day is about all you can move a herd. So this pass saved stockmen a couple of days going or coming, not to mention the weight animals lose from being driven extra miles from one range to another."

Hildy nodded. "So now we know Mr. Kessick's reason for wanting the ranch. I can see why it would be to his advantage if Uncle Nate couldn't make the mortgage payment. Mr. Kessick would then own this place. But why'd he burn the barn down and cut the wire?"

The old ranger gave his mustache a flip. "Now hold on, Hildy. It seems certain that's what happened, but we have no proof Kessick's riders did it."

"It had to be!" Ruby cried. "Nobody else had a reason."

"Maybe so," Brother Ben replied, "but you can't go accusing a man without proof. That's what we've got to have—proof."

Ruby protested. "How we a-gonna do that, huh? We got to be lookin' fer my pa."

"We're going to do both," the old ranger said. "Now, if you'll help unload the supplies I brought for Mrs. Benton, we can get on with our investigation."

A few minutes later, after Mrs. Benton had thanked them repeatedly for the supplies, the old ranger led the others back to the car. Shifting the big white hat on the back of his head, he looked at The Pass. "It's only about three miles through there," he said. "I ort to be able to follow the tracks of cows and horses. When I catch up with the riders, I can find out who they're working for."

"Shouldn't we be a-lookin' fer my father fust?" Ruby argued.

The old man shook his head. "We got no clue where to even start looking for him. But maybe those night riders can give us a hint. 'Course, it'd be safer if I didn't have to walk."

"Safer?" Hildy asked in alarm. "Do you think those riders will hurt you when you catch up to them?"

"It's not the riders that concern me, Hildy. This is rattlesnake country. When the stock passed through this morning, it was cool, so there wouldn't likely be a problem. Rattlesnakes like warmth, and right now they'll be active." He thought for a moment. "My boots are enough protection if I'm careful," he added.

Hildy started to say, "Please don't go!" but stopped when she saw the look on Ruby's face. "Then let me go with you," Hildy suggested.

Spud shook his head. "You girls stay," he ordered. "You don't have boots. I do, so I'll go. If we catch up to those riders, it'd be better if I was there with Mr. Strong."

The old ranger gave his mustache a flip and smiled at Hildy. "See what I meant earlier about the look in this young man's eyes? Come to think of it, you've got that same look, Hildy."

Hildy was pleased, but before she could reply, Ben Strong motioned to Spud. Settling his wide-brimmed hat on his head, he walked beside the old ranger. Hildy watched anxiously as they approached the buckeye and manzanita growing among the rocks and boulders at the mouth of The Pass.

Spud and the old ranger hadn't gone twenty feet inside the high black walls when both stopped suddenly.

Ruby froze. "Reckon they's a-seein' snakes a-ready?"

Hildy nodded, watching the old man point ahead, then to the left. Spud pointed to his right, then slowly, man and boy backed up.

When they again neared the cut fence, Spud called out. "Rattlers everywhere! Buzzing like mad, too. In all my hoboing, this New York City boy never saw anything like that."

Ben Strong rested his hand on Spud's shoulder. "Since we can't follow the night riders' tracks, Hildy, why don't you reclaim your raccoon and let's ask at ranch houses about Ruby's father."

Throughout the afternoon, they questioned the few residents in the open, barren country. Hildy was sorry she'd brought Mischief. It was too hot in the car, even with the windows down, so Hildy had to carry the raccoon. When they got out to ask questions at a remote ranch house, Mischief wiggled uncomfortably in the hot sun.

Hildy was concerned, too, because of the dull dynamite explosions they heard in the distance. After one extra-loud blast from the dam, she jumped. "They must be blowing up whole mountainsides."

"We're safe as long as we don't get close to where they're

blasting," the old ranger assured them as they stopped at another lonely house on a barren hill.

A young housewife peered through the sagging, rusted screen door with rags stuck in holes to keep out flies. Hildy could see a child in the woman's arms, and several small children clung to her tattered skirts or peered from behind her.

The pale young woman looked at Ruby's sepia-tone snapshot and raised her eyebrows. "Don't know his name," she answered Ruby's usual question. "Seed him 'round some, though."

"Where?" Ruby seemed to breathe the word.

"When he was fixin' to raise that barn some time back. Tall, skinny feller, he was. At first, some of us—like my husbun'—offered to he'p, but he didn't want none. Polite, he was, but said he'd do it hisself. He kept to hisself all the time. Everybody at the Grange Hall at Crane's Crossing"—she waved toward the south—"and even at the Legion Hall there, they all figured he was kinda strange. None of us ever really talked to him, I guess."

Ben Strong touched the brim of his white hat. "We're obliged, ma'am. Is there anybody else around these parts who might have known this man?"

The woman shook her head. "Nope. That feller built that place alone. With ropes, pulleys, skids, and a horse—he done it all. 'Ceptin' the high parts. The sheepherder he'ped him on them."

"Sheepherder?" Hildy asked.

"Seen him only at a distance, but that's what he had to be. At the Grange meetin', others said the same thing. Wasn't nobody we knowed, and there was that smell—you know, like a sheep camp gits. And sheepherders."

Ben Strong smiled. "Where can we find this sheepherder?"

The woman shrugged. "I ain't got no idee. When that strange, skinny man and the herder finished the barn about three months ago, they both disappeared. Ain't seen hide ner hair of either since."

Later that day, on the drive back to the valley, Hildy held Mischief in her lap while everyone discussed what they'd learned.

The old ranger summed it up. "At least one person—a sheep-herder—knew Nate Konning enough to work with him. But how'd a cowboy like Mr. Konning get to be friends with a sheepherder? Even that poor woman back there, hardly looking like she had two pennies to her name, looked down her nose at sheepherders."

"Well," Hildy said, "at least that herder's somebody we can look for when we come back up here. Maybe he can tell us where Uncle Nate is."

Brother Ben nodded. "I'd like to take you kids up here again, but I'm going to be tied up with some real estate business for a while."

Ruby slumped dejectedly in her seat. "I hate anythin' that keeps me from a-lookin' fer my daddy," she complained.

Spud changed the subject. "How about dropping me off at my place first so all of you can see the tree house I built?"

Hildy and Ben Strong liked the idea, but Ruby didn't say anything. She stared moodily out the open car window.

It was almost sundown when they reached the Pattmans' chicken ranch where Spud lived.

"Oh no!" Hildy exclaimed as the Packard turned into the driveway. "There's the Jarmans' pickup! They're the ones who threatened to hurt Mischief."

Spud chuckled and pointed. "Look at Lindy. He's not letting them out of the car. The Pattmans must not be home."

The old ranger stopped the car and turned around to talk to the girls. "Since we have Mischief with us, perhaps we'd better let Spud walk from here and talk to them. Hildy, I'll drive you and the coon home. Ruby, too."

Hildy shook her head. "No, thanks. I want to see Spud's tree house, and I also want to find out what the Jarmans are doing here."

Ruby roused from her silence. "Ye kin be shore it ain't nothin' nice fer you ner yore coon, Hildy," she muttered.

CHAPTER
TEN

—

UNBELIEVABLE NEWS

Spud leaned out of the right front window as Ben Strong eased the Packard even with the Star. "Down, Lindy! Stay!" he shouted.

The dog dropped obediently into the dust.

Charley Jarman got out of the pickup, tugged at his overall straps and bent to peer inside the Packard's front seat. He didn't see Hildy, Ruby, and Mischief in the backseat. They were partly hidden by the afternoon shadows.

The coon hunter ran his rough hand along the plush upholstery behind the old ranger's head. "Whooeee!" he exclaimed. "Ain't this here a purdy sight, Rafe?"

The boy played with the spotlight outside the driver's side. "Shore is! An' lookee here at this here ol' spotlight, Pa! Don't ye reckon we'uns could see a coon in the highest branch of any tree as ever growed if'n we had this?"

Hildy's anger rose quickly. She wanted to give that man a good tongue thrashing.

The old ranger seemed to anticipate her. "You two girls stay put," he whispered. Opening the door, he stepped out, gently placing himself between the uncouth man and his son. Spud slid out the other side and hurried around the car to stand by the old ranger.

"What kinda car is that?" Rafe asked.

"A 1929 Packard 645 Victoria," Brother Strong said in his easy drawl. "Straight eight. Bought it just before the Crash of twenty-nine. Glad you like it." He smiled. "Why don't we all step over here in the shade of this walnut tree where we can talk?"

"Who're you, Mister?" Charley Jarman demanded but in a slightly more polite tone than he'd used a moment before. Hildy sensed that the old ranger's confident bearing, height, and soft-spokenness had somewhat intimidated the coon hunter.

"Name's Ben Strong." The old ranger removed his hat and immediately resettled it on his thatch of snow-white hair.

Hildy wondered if the gesture was meant to be polite while avoiding shaking the other man's filthy hand.

"The land man?" Mr. Jarman asked, his voice definitely taking on a touch of awe. "Reckon y'all're one o' the richest fellers in these here parts."

"I'm comfortable," the old ranger replied, leading the way to the walnut tree's shade a short distance away.

Spud snapped his fingers, and immediately Lindy surged to his feet and followed.

Ben Strong cleared his throat. "You and your son looking for anyone in particular?" he asked.

Rafe's mouth dropped open. "You live here, Mr. Strong?" The boy's hand swept toward the chicken house, which was being used as a dwelling.

His father kicked the boy on his ankle bone. Rafe grabbed it and jumped about. "Ouch!" he cried. "Why'd ye do that fer?"

Hildy almost laughed because Brother Ben didn't seem to notice. He answered the other man's question. "My young friend lives here." He nodded toward Spud. "He works for the Pattmans. They live there." He indicated the chicken house. "I'm sure Spud wouldn't mind you answering my questions, Mr. Jarman."

"No," Spud said emphatically. "In fact, I insist on it! And I'd like total veracity, please."

In the backseat, Hildy couldn't suppress a giggle. "Got to remember to look that word up, Ruby," she whispered.

Ruby made a face. "Him and his two-dollar words," she grumbled.

"Shh!" Hildy scolded. "I want to hear them."

Mr. Jarman studied Spud through half-closed eyes, then turned to the tall old man. "Me'n muh boy was a-comin' to ask these here neighbors if'n they been losin' aigs from the hen house, same's us. But nobody's home here."

The coon hunter pointed toward the Corrigans' barn-house. "We know they's a mean coon over yonder. Fust off, it like to a-kilt my pappy hound. Now it's stealin' our aigs what me'n muh boy depend on to keep alive durin' these hard times."

Rafe shoved his hands into the pockets of his grimy overalls. "Aigs an' critters we ketch with our dawgs—coons and 'possum an' such like," he added.

Hildy reached for the car door, intending to jump out and defend Mischief. She froze when she heard Spud's sudden, explosive reply.

"I know the Corrigans!" His short temper flared, and his face turned red. "Mischief didn't tackle your worthless mongrel!" His voice was hard and flat, landing on ears like openhanded slaps. "She didn't eat your eggs, either! But it's not uncommon for dogs to do that when they're hungry. So why don't you look to your own hounds as possibly responsible? They could be egg-sucking dogs, for all I know!"

Hildy and Ruby looked at each other, surprised at the intensity of Spud's outburst.

Mr. Jarman closed one eye and squinted at Spud through the other.

"Now I 'member you, boy! Well, y'all got yorself a powerful friend in Mr. Strong here. Howsomever, he won't always be along to perteck ye nor yore girlfriend with the long pigtails nor her dumb blond friend."

Ruby let out a loud screech. Before Hildy could stop her, Ruby burst from the backseat and rushed upon the Jarmans like a runaway buzz saw. "Dumb, am I? Take that!" She started swinging. "An' that! An' that!" She kicked, punched, slapped, and swung wildly in one mad blur of motion.

Charley Jarman and his son retreated toward their converted pickup, and Ruby chased after them.

Hildy jumped out of the Packard. "Ruby, no!" she yelled. "Stop it!"

Lindy jumped up and bounded after Mr. Jarman. Just as the dog was about to attack the coon hunter, Spud's sharp command stopped him. Spud ran up and pulled the Airedale off.

Ben Strong outran Hildy to reach Ruby first. Coming up from behind, the old ranger clamped Ruby's hands to her sides and lifted the kicking and screaming girl away from her victims.

"Let me go!" Ruby hollered. "Let me go!"

The old ranger carried her quickly to the Packard. Spud dashed past and jerked the back door open. Brother Strong placed her solidly on the backseat and closed the door.

Hildy glanced in alarm at the old ranger, but for all his eighty-five years, he didn't even seem to be breathing hard.

"Watch her, please, Hildy," he said quietly, then turned toward the Jarmans.

They were already inside the Star, and the coupe lurched forward, spinning its wheels in the dust. In seconds, the driver headed toward the county road. As he sped past, he sprayed a vile stream of tobacco juice over the Packard's right front spare wheel. "Now y'all done it!" he yelled out the window. "I'll git even!" Then he was gone in a rooster tail of dust.

Hildy gazed thoughtfully after the Jarmans' old vehicle. "I'm sorry about this, Brother Strong," she said. "I didn't want you to become involved in my problems with those two people."

"I've had real troubles in my life, Hildy. Forget those people," the old man replied with a flip of his mustache. "Now, Spud, let's finish the tour of your tree house you promised us."

Spud motioned to the girls. "Come on, Hildy. Ruby. Leave the coon and come see!"

Hildy looked at Ruby. Her cousin's fury was gone. Ruby nodded and both girls got out of the car.

As they approached the tree trunk, Spud pointed to some

pieces of wood nailed into the tree trunk. "See these steps?" he said. "Made them myself. Goes right up to my door. It's real oak. Found it in an old house somebody was tearing down along the river."

Hildy waited with Ruby and Lindy until Spud and the old ranger had climbed about ten feet up to where four huge limbs branched off in different directions. Then, tucking her long dress about her knees as ladylike as possible, Hildy followed. Ruby, dressed in overalls, climbed rapidly as the man and boy had done.

Spud stopped at the top of the crude steps. "The building is about twenty feet long," he said with pride. "It's eight feet high and twelve feet deep. I sometimes have to duck my head when I'm climbing up into the loft where I've made my bed, but you'll see that even Mr. Strong can stand on the wooden floor in the middle without having to bend over."

Hildy looked up. "It's much bigger than it looks from the ground."

"Wait'll you get inside," Spud continued, climbing through the doorway. "There're three windows. This one in the door is four feet by four feet. The second window is in a door that's turned sideways and used as part of the wall behind my bed. The third one is on the far side of the house, above the bunk. So two windows face the front and one faces the back. There're no curtains over the windows, though, I'm afraid." As the others approached the doorway, he helped them up. "Come in. It's a little snug, but there's room for everyone."

Hildy stepped into the room behind Brother Ben, and her eyes quickly surveyed the room. Not an inch of space had been wasted.

A two-burner flat-top wood stove stood just inside the door. The black chimney rose straight up in front of the door, so everyone had to walk around it to enter.

Hildy glanced at Spud, and he shrugged. "We're not talking safety," he admitted. "But it cooks my meals. When the lids are hot, I lift them off with this piece of metal. Stove makes the place very warm this time of year, especially in my bunk, which is up high."

Hildy looked around the room curiously. There was only one piece of free-standing furniture—a black three-legged milk stool with a back had been pushed against a built-in pine desk. Spud pointed out that there was just enough room above the desk for two nailed-on steps that led to the loft and the full-sized bed.

"I store food on top of the desk," he added, pointing to a couple of cans and a few bottles. "Sorry there isn't any furniture for you to sit on, but there are throw pillows by the bookcases under the bed. You girls can pull the pillows out and sit on them if you want. Mr. Strong, you can take the milk stool."

As they complied, Hildy noticed that two library shelves had been built in under the bed's loft. On the shelves there was a Bible, *Selected Works of Shakespeare,* Homer's *Odyssey* and *The Iliad,* plus Jack London's *Call of the Wild.* Several dime novel westerns were neatly stacked on the lower shelf. Hildy wondered if Spud missed the dictionary he had loaned her.

Spud climbed the stairs by the desk and sat in the loft, his feet dangling over the side of the bed.

As they all sat there silently for a few moments, Hildy noticed a slight musty smell. She decided it probably came from the huge cardboard boxes that had been used to line the inside walls. They had pictures of Mickey Mouse on one side and the words, *Post Toasties Corn Flakes* on the other.

Spud apparently saw her nose wrinkle. "When I finished the house, I took a hose and washed the dust off the outside," he explained with a wry smile. "But I'd forgotten to caulk it, so it got wet inside. Later I caulked it inside and out by mashing up old newspapers. Nailed these big cartons into place for insulation, too. Better'n newspapers, like some people have instead of wallpaper."

Hildy smiled. "My Granny Dunnigan has old newspapers for wallpaper, back in the Ozarks," she said. For a moment, a sad, lonely feeling washed over her as she thought about her grandmother.

Someday, Hildy told herself silently, *I've got to go back and see her. Maybe if Ruby finds her father—I mean—when Ruby finds her father, we can all go back together. Maybe Ruby and I can even get our two grandmothers to speak to each other after all these years. After all, they are sisters.*

But that wasn't likely, Hildy decided, since Granny hadn't answered her letter. Hildy thought about writing again, but stamps cost three cents each. Molly couldn't afford to give Hildy money for stamps, and Hildy couldn't get work in the area.

Hildy thought about an article she had recently read in the local newspaper about the hard times. Millions of men couldn't get work of any kind, and those who did averaged only seventeen dollars a week. That meant less than nine hundred dollars a year for a man to care for his family.

A hired farmhand made just over two hundred a year, which was the bottom of the scale. Hildy thought her father made better than that working as a cowboy from sunup to sundown, but she heard that coal miners made just over seven hundred dollars a year. She was glad her father wasn't a coal miner, though, risking his life twelve months a year.

Spud broke off something he was saying to look out the front door window. "Somebody's coming," he said, raising one eyebrow. "I think it's Brother Hyde."

By the time the pastor stopped his black Chevrolet sedan in the dusty driveway, everyone had climbed down from the tree house.

Brother Hyde, a nice-looking man with a gentle face, slid out of the car, straightening his wire-rimmed glasses on his nose.

"I hoped I'd find at least one of you here," he began with a hearty smile. He walked over and shook hands with Brother Strong, then Spud, Hildy, and Ruby.

The minister, in his early fifties, always wore a dark hat and blue serge suit with shiny pants, even in summer. The cuffs on his pants frayed around the edges, and the heels of his plain black shoes were run-down.

Hildy hadn't read what a local church pastor earned, but a priest received slightly more than eight hundred dollars a year. Hildy doubted that Brother Hyde was paid that much, although he certainly deserved that or more.

The minister brushed some dust off his pants. "I came because Brother Kensington—you all know him—took some baskets up to Mrs. Benton this afternoon," he explained. "He just got back and when he stopped by the parsonage, he said that you folks had visited Mrs. Benton that morning. So you must know about the fire?"

When everyone nodded, the pastor continued. "Brother Kensington's radiator boiled dry on the way back, so he stopped at a small stream near Thunder Mountain. He took a can down to the creek to get water for his car, and there he saw a couple of boys about twelve or so."

Hildy listened impatiently, wondering what this was all about.

"They were panning for gold to buy their school clothes," the pastor said. "And these boys told Brother Kensington that they knew a sheepherder who'd helped build a barn at The Pass. The herder had a friend whose description matched that of Nate Konning."

Ruby yelped. "They know whar my daddy is?"

"I didn't say that, Ruby," Brother Hyde said calmly. "What the boys told Brother Kensington was that they knew where to find the sheepherder who had helped build the barn. The boys didn't know where to find the man that answers your father's description."

Hildy sat up straight. "Then let's go talk to this other man," she suggested. "Maybe he can tell us where to find Uncle Nate."

The pastor smiled. "I thought that's what you'd say. I'm going to drive up that way tomorrow. Would you girls like to come along?"

After the excited girls quieted down, the pastor cleared his throat and looked at Ruby. "I don't know how to say this, but . . ."

"Spit it out!" Ruby exclaimed.

"Well, uh . . . the boys who were panning for gold seemed quite sure that this other man—apparently Nate Konning, who's always been a cowboy—is now working as a . . . uh . . ."

"Sheepherder," Brother Strong finished quietly. "I figured it out that way. Nate Konning is a sheepherder."

CHAPTER
ELEVEN

—

TROUBLE IN LONE RIVER

That ain't so!" Ruby cried, her eyes blazing. "My pa's a cowboy. He wouldn't never be no sheepherder!"

Hildy reached out and touched her cousin's arm. "Don't get upset, Ruby. You yourself told those boys at Simple Justice that sheepherding was honest work, remember? You said that King David had been a shepherd boy. And you offered to give Rob Kessick a knuckle sandwich for insulting the Bible."

"This's diff'runt!" Ruby protested.

Brother Hyde rested his hand on her shoulder. "Ruby, it's too bad you couldn't have heard my sermon about the Prodigal Son," he said gently.

"I learned all them ol' stories when I was a little girl," Ruby said. "I don't need to hear no more, 'specially not that one!"

Hildy took a slow breath and let it out before speaking. "I think what Brother Hyde's saying is that your father may have been forced to do what that Prodigal Son did," she said. "The Prodigal Son was a Jew, so he couldn't even eat a pig. Yet he got so far down in life that he had to feed pigs in order to live.

So if your father couldn't get a job riding in these hard times, maybe he had no choice but to become a sheepherder."

Ruby started to protest again, then slowly shook her head. "If'n he's really my daddy, then I don't keer what he is—long's I kin find him."

"That's the spirit, Ruby." The pastor grinned. "Well, let's see what we can find out tomorrow."

Brother Strong stopped at the Slaytons' house where Ruby was living, and she told them that she was going to stay overnight with Hildy. While she was there, Ruby picked up her only pair of shoes. The day's experience in the hills with the old ranger had convinced both girls they should wear shoes in case they went walking.

On the sixth day since they had met Ozzell Kessick and found clues to the whereabouts of Ruby's father, both girls awoke at dawn. They were eager for the ride to the foothills with Brother Hyde.

As they got dressed and put their shoes on, they talked excitedly about what they might find out that day. Ruby was fastening her overall straps and Hildy was finishing braiding her hair when Elizabeth came racing into the barn-house.

"Car coming! Car coming!" Hildy's younger sister cried.

"Brother Hyde's early!" Hildy exclaimed, hurrying to tie a white string at the end of her long brown braids.

"It's not the preacher," Elizabeth announced. "It's a man I don't know."

Hildy and Ruby ran to the sliding barn door and peered out the small window. Hildy had been trying to learn all the different kinds of cars that mixed with buggies and spring wagons in the area. "It's a Whippet sedan," she said.

"Do ye reco'nize the driver?" Ruby asked.

When Hildy shook her head, Molly went to the door. "I'll go see who it is," she offered. "Hildy, you keep an eye on Joey. Don't let Mischief steal the baby's cracker."

Hildy's stepmother slid the barn door open a little and walked through, trailed by Elizabeth, Martha, Sarah, and Iola. Ruby sat down at the table while Hildy turned back to check her baby brother. He was tied to a straight-backed chair with a dishtowel so he wouldn't fall over. Mischief prowled around the mattresses where the girls slept.

Since the girls left the sliding door partly open, Hildy and Ruby could see some of what was going on and hear the conversation. "Mrs. Corrigan?" the stranger asked, stepping off the running board onto the dirt. "I'm Albert Featherstone. I live down the road about a quarter mile."

"Oh, Mr. Featherstone, I'm glad to know you. I've been wanting to thank you for phoning the fire department when our place here was burning."

Mr. Featherstone smiled. "Glad the volunteers got here in time to save the place," he said. "Having a phone comes in handy, like now. Your preacher just called and asked me if I'd bring your daughter a message."

"Hildy's getting dressed. May I give it to her?"

"That'd be fine," Mr. Featherstone replied. "He says an emergency came up, and he won't be able to take the girls to the mountains today. But he'll do it tomorrow, same time."

Disappointed, Hildy looked over at her cousin.

Ruby's face mirrored her deep hurt. "Tomorry'll be a full week gone," she complained. "Seems like nothin's goin' right fer me to find my daddy." She threw herself face down on the girls' mattress.

"Watch out!" Hildy cried, but it was too late.

Mischief shot out from under the pillow with a biscuit in her mouth.

"Dumb coon!" Ruby muttered. "What's she a-doin' in the bed?"

Hildy smiled. "Stealing food Elizabeth's been hiding again," Hildy replied. She watched as Mischief recovered her dignity, crossed to the washbasin on the stand and began vigorously washing the biscuit. "Oh no, Mischief!" Hildy cried. "It'll melt away . . . Oh, well."

Mischief soon made little complaining noises and felt around in the water for the biscuit. It had mysteriously disappeared.

When Molly and the girls reappeared, Hildy's little sisters

bounced up and down with excitement.

"Tell 'em, Molly," Martha urged, clapping her hands.

"I'm going to, girls. Hildy, Ruby, that was Mr. Featherstone, and—"

"We heard," Ruby said glumly. "Brother Hyde cain't take us a-lookin' fer my daddy today."

"But," Sarah broke in, "Mr. Featherstone says he's going shopping for school clothes today with his missus and their son. He said we could go, too. So, would you help us get dressed, Hildy, huh, wouldja?"

Hildy started to answer, but Molly bent over quickly and pulled her little stepdaughter close. "You misunderstood, Sarah. There isn't room in Mr. Featherstone's car for all of us. Besides, you're only five. You can't start school until next year."

Sarah let out a disappointed wail, but stopped short at the sound of an anguished squall from Elizabeth on the other side of the room.

"Who messed up my pillow?" Elizabeth demanded. She ran over and felt under the worn pillow, which had no pillowcase. None of the pillows did. There were no sheets, either, just the pale blue-and-white striped mattresses and pillows.

"It's gone!" Elizabeth cried, straightening up. "Oh, that raccoon! She's taken the biscuit I hid. Sometimes I wish those mean old Jarmans would catch her!"

Hildy whirled to face her sister. "Don't ever say that!" Hildy scolded. "Not even joking."

When the girls had calmed down and were laughing about the biscuit washing, Ruby announced she didn't feel like going shopping. She volunteered to keep Sarah, Iola, and the baby so Molly could just take the three older girls, who would attend school in September. "I'll keep me an eye on Mischief, too," she offered. "There shore ain't a-gonna be room fer a coon in the car."

Although they took Ruby up on her offer, the Whippet was packed with seven people when Mr. Featherstone later drove the shoppers into town. He was a short, balding man with a red face, and his wife looked as round as a sausage. Their seven-year-old son, who seemed small for his age, sat on his mother's lap in front, never opening his mouth.

In town, Hildy glanced around, her eyes hungry to notice things. Everywhere she looked, Hildy saw the familiar Blue Eagle and the words *NRA Member. We Do Our Part.*

Hildy had heard about the NRA. It stood for National Recovery Administration. It was one of many "alphabet agencies" President Franklin D. Roosevelt had started since taking office the year before, when he defeated Herbert Hoover. All the agencies were supposed to help put people back to work. In a nation where there were few jobs, the "alphabet agencies" offered hope.

Molly walked past the dime store, which advertised "Nothing Over Forty-nine Cents." Molly, Hildy, Elizabeth, and Martha trailed Mrs. Featherstone and her son to a clothing store next door. A sign in the window read "Boys' Cotton Slacks, $1.59; Shoes, $2.95; Girls' Dresses, Sizes 7–14, $1.95 to $2.95."

Martha tugged on Molly's sleeve. "Can I have two dresses, huh?"

Molly patted the youngster on the head. "You know the rule," she said. "I'll make two dresses for each of you girls—one for school and one for church. You can each buy two pair of shoes. One for school and the other for Sunday."

As soon as they walked in the door, the store owner waddled over to them with a smile. He was a short, heavy-set man with a bald pate and ring of curly blond hair from there back. "May I help you?" he asked politely.

Molly nodded. "Yes, thank you. I need shoes for each of my three girls."

"If you'll step this way . . ." The owner's voice trailed off when the small bell over the door tinkled and a matronly woman bustled in.

Her stylishly short hair peaked out from under the prettiest hat Hildy had ever seen. Hildy loved to look at hats in the Sears & Roebuck catalog. Most of them were 79 cents to $1.98. But this hat must have cost at least twelve dollars—as much as some men's suits. The rest of the woman's wardrobe looked equally expensive in a time when money was scarce.

"Excuse me," the storeowner said to Molly. Turning away, he hurried across the wooden floor. "Ah, Mrs. Ring! How nice to see you again. What may I show you?"

A warm flush stole over Hildy's face, but a quick glance at Molly showed she was even more embarrassed.

Elizabeth stomped her foot. "Hey, mister!" she cried. "We were here first."

The wealthy woman turned haughtily and tipped her head back slightly so she could see better from under the stylish wide brim. "Okies!" she said with distaste.

Though strongly opinionated, Hildy wasn't given to sudden outbursts of anger like Ruby. Yet in that instant, the woman's remark stung Hildy like a willow switch across bare skin. Her face flaming at the insult, she swallowed hard, fighting a powerful urge to shout back.

Molly took a deep breath. "Come on, girls," she said quickly in a small, tight voice. "Let's get out of here."

Hildy hesitated, furious over the rude remark yet unsure what she should do.

Suddenly she heard a man's voice behind her. "Don't let it bother you, folks," he told them.

Hildy turned to see Ben Strong stepping out from a small cubicle that had a curtain in front. The old ranger held a handsome, three-piece blue wool suit. Hildy was close enough to read the price tag. It said $31.50.

"I couldn't help but overhear," he went on, tipping his white cowboy hat. "I'm sorry. Seems some folks have money, but no manners. If you'd like, Sister Corrigan, I'll drive you folks to another store—"

The owner shuffled quickly across the wooden floor. "Oh, Mr. Strong, if these people are friends of yours—"

"They are!" the old ranger replied a little shortly. "Here's the suit I tried on. I don't believe I'll buy anything today." He reached over and took Molly's arm. "May I escort you out?"

Tears sprang to Hildy's eyes, and a bitter taste filled her mouth. Yet at the same time, she wanted to laugh or cheer or something—anything to express the mixture of feelings that flooded her whole being.

Outside the store, Hildy grabbed the old ranger's other arm. "Brother Ben," she said proudly, "that was about the nicest thing anybody ever did for us."

Molly nodded. "Thank you," she murmured in barely a whisper. Her face was still red from embarrassment.

Hildy and the others turned to look through the plate glass window. The storeowner still stood where they had left him while the well-dressed woman shook her finger at him across the counter.

Elizabeth shook her head. "Serves him right," she muttered. "I hope he goes broke . . . ignoring us to wait on that rich lady!"

The old ranger fingered his mustache and steered Molly toward his yellow Packard, parked next to the Featherstones' car. "They used to call me things like that—and worse," he said in his soft, easy drawl. "It hurts, but it won't do permanent damage unless you let it."

Elizabeth frowned up at the tall, stately man. "Did people really call you names, Brother Ben?"

He nodded. "When I came to California, I was dead busted broke. I'd lost everything and wasn't young anymore. I had an accent, which you may've noticed. I had been a lot of things in life—"

"I know," Elizabeth interrupted. "The folks at church told us about you. You were a Civil War vet and an Indian fighter and a Texas Ranger and a U.S. Marshall in Oklahoma!"

"Oklahoma was a territory when I did that," the old man added gently. "But none of that counted when I arrived here. That was before all the thousands of Dust Bowl refugees started pouring in here as they have been the last couple years. There's a lot more resentment now, and it's bound to get worse. But don't be upset—any of you. You're quality folks."

Tears filled Molly's eyes. "Thank you," she whispered.

The old man looked away.

"What happened, Brother Ben?" Elizabeth asked. "I mean, what made people quit calling you names like they just did us.

How come they treat you with respect now? Is it because you're rich?"

Hildy grabbed her sister's arm and gave it a warning yank.

The old ranger didn't seem to notice. He smiled down at Elizabeth from his great height. "Strange as it seems, money follows. It's never first. You may be a little young to under-stand—"

Hildy broke in quickly. "I don't understand that, either, Brother Ben, but I'd like to. Will you explain it, please?"

"If you're really interested—of course, Hildy."

"I'm interested!" she said emphatically. "I'm never again going to be called 'Okie' or anything else that sounds bad. Nei-ther's my family."

"That's the stuff." The old ranger smiled and reached out impulsively to touch the girl's shoulder. "Decision and deter-mination is where it all starts. But there's more you need to know. Maybe we can talk about it another time." He turned to Molly. "Sister Corrigan, would you like me to take you some-where?"

"Oh, thank you, but we're with neighbors." Molly pointed to the car beside his. "The Featherstones gave us a lift. Thanks, anyway." Molly reached out and took the old ranger's hand. "Thank you again—for everything!"

―――――――

That afternoon inside the barn-house, Hildy, Molly, Eliza-beth, and Martha told Ruby what had happened in town.

Ruby exploded. "I'd a liked to a-been thar! I'd a whupped that nasty old hen so hard she'd never want to call nobody a name never agin!"

Hildy hid a smile behind her hand, but it vanished as five-year-old Sarah dashed inside the sliding door, her eyes wide and her face pale. "Come quick!" she cried. "Something terri-ble's happened to Missy!"

CHAPTER
TWELVE

—

SOMEONE'S FOLLOWING

Hildy gasped. "What's happened to Mischief?" she exclaimed.

"Come see," Sarah replied, dashing back out the barn door.

Hildy and Ruby rushed after the five-year-old as she ran barefoot in front of the barn, heading for the west end by the clover pasture. The others followed, and Molly brought up the rear, holding the baby in her arms.

Hildy's heart thumped wildly. "If Mr. Jarman or his son hurt Mischief . . ."

Ruby ran alongside her cousin. "That thar coon was jist fine a few minutes ago," she said. "Mischief wasn't outta my sight all the time ye was in town!"

The older girls outran Sarah and rounded the western end of the barn together. Suddenly they stopped. The raccoon was nowhere in sight.

Hildy and Ruby looked around frantically. Sarah ran a few steps past them and stopped. Turning around, she pointed. "Up there! On the roof!"

Hildy tilted her head back to see where her little sister was pointing, then sucked her breath in sharply.

Mischief sat near the middle of the barn's highest peak. Fresh blood clearly showed on her nose and across the light-colored hairs on her face.

"She's hurt," Hildy moaned. "Oh, Mischief!"

"It musta jist happened!" Ruby exclaimed.

Hildy shaded her eyes against the sun's glare. "Come down, Mischief. Come on. Let's see what happened so I can help fix it."

Usually, the raccoon came as readily as a dog or cat when called, but not this time. Mischief sat in a sad, huddled mass, her long, ringed tail wrapped around her body. She silently stared down at Hildy and the others.

Hildy turned around. "Where's the ladder?" she asked. "I've got to go up and get her."

"No, Hildy!" Molly's voice was firm. "It's too risky for you to climb up there. You could slip and kill yourself."

"But, Molly! I've got to help Mischief and she won't come down!"

"I'm sorry, Hildy. You'll just have to wait until she comes down on her own."

Hildy started to protest, but Ruby grabbed her arm hard.

"Lookee yonder on that thar' fence by the clover field!" Ruby pointed. "Reckon that's what hurt Mischief."

Trying to decide what she would do to the Jarmans for hurting her pet, Hildy gazed in the direction Ruby's finger pointed.

On top of the two-by-four frame for the small chicken-wire gate sat a large yellow cat with white forepaws and a large white patch on his chest. Calmly, he licked his left front paw.

"They's blood on his chest," Ruby said. "See it? An' on his right forepaw, too. I bet that's Mischief's blood!"

Although momentarily relieved that Mr. Jarman or his son hadn't hurt her raccoon, a sudden wave of anger washed over her. She rushed toward the cat.

"Don't, Hildy!" Ruby cried, grabbing her cousin's forearm. "I reckon that thar ol' tomcat's the one that cut up Mr. Jarman's pappy houn' dawg, too. He's a mighty big cat to come up on without a broom or somethin'."

Hildy hesitated, still seething inside. How could that cat just sit there, totally unconcerned? All the loud voices should have clearly warned him that he was in danger.

Molly clutched the baby close to her and stood next to Hildy. "Ruby's right, Hildy," she said. "That cat is no more afraid of us than he was of your little coon. Leave him alone and he'll go away."

"But he'll come back," Hildy protested. "And maybe he'll do worse things to Mischief."

"Better leave him alone," Molly repeated. "Wait until your father gets home. He'll know what to do."

"But we don't know where that cat lives or if he even belongs to anybody," Hildy replied. "So many people can't feed a pet these days that maybe he's just on his own—gone wild!"

"Just the same," Molly said evenly, "I'm afraid to bother him. Let's go around on the other side of the barn-house and see if we can coax Mischief down. Maybe the tomcat'll be gone by then."

The girls obeyed, but the raccoon stayed on the roof until well after dark. Hildy treated Mischief's wounds with peroxide, which foamed as she poured it on the cuts. The raccoon didn't want to go out that night, and Hildy spent anxious hours wondering how to deal with this new danger to her pet.

The next morning when Pastor Hyde arrived, he said Hildy could take Mischief along on the ride up to Thunder Mountain. Both girls wore shoes and took wide-brimmed straw hats in case they had to walk in the boiling sun. Spud came prepared, too, wearing his cowboy hat and boots.

Hildy was relieved about being able to take the raccoon along but a little concerned about the big tomcat's threat to the rest of her family.

Spud and Ruby assured her that the cat was not likely to bother the Corrigan kids as long as they left him alone. Hildy relaxed, then, and tried to enjoy the ride into the foothills.

At Shaw's Ferry, Pastor Hyde stopped at the town's only store and bought two quarts of fresh milk. Then he drove on to the sod house at the foot of Thunder Mountain.

When they arrived at the sod house, Hildy thought Mrs.

Benton looked a little pale. But the widow seemed to brighten as Hildy introduced the pastor to her and her family. The children stared silently at the pastor, then turned their attention to the raccoon.

Hildy quickly explained the coon's wounds. "Looks as if that tomcat just took one swipe across Mischief's nose. But a cat's claws are sharp, and Mischief is very sore and tender."

Seven-year-old Rachel edged up to the raccoon. "Could we just hold her then . . . if we're real careful?"

Hildy read the longing in the eyes of Rachel as well as her brother and sisters. "All right," she gave in. "But be very, very gentle."

The children agreed, so Hildy handed Mischief over to Rachel.

Ruby and Spud reached into the Packard and lifted out the quart bottles of milk. Through the clear glass, Hildy eyed the rich cream that had risen to the top of the narrow neck.

Mrs. Benton gratefully accepted the gift. "Thankee kindly, everybody," she said. "I hate takin' charity, but my kids got to eat. The baby's been getting by on canned condensed milk. The older ones done without." She smiled down at her youngest. "I been thinkin' about weaning Becky off that bottle, but she's liable not to git enough to eat if I do that. She sure needs fresh milk like this. Thankee agin."

The minister nodded. "There's a milk war in Sacramento," he replied. "Price is down to seven cents a quart and expected to drop to six cents. That's forcing the price down in this area, too."

"We coulda brought more," Ruby said, "but none of us knowed if'n ye had any way of keepin' it from spoilin' in this heat. We didn't see no well."

The pastor added, "We doubted the ice man delivers out here."

"No, he don't," the widow said. "Anyhow, we ain't got no icebox. So we'll do what other folks do hereabouts—put it in the shade and drink it afore it spoils. 'Course, ain't no shade here 'ceptin' jist close to the sod house."

She handed the bottles to her son. "Cover 'em good to keep out the flies."

While Jacob hurried away, the pastor spoke quietly to the boy's mother. "We thought perhaps you had enough food for a while, Mrs. Benton, but if you need school clothes—"

"Mercy! You folks have been too kind already. Besides, my young'uns ain't had a whole lot of schoolin' the last year."

The minister nodded in understanding. "Do you attend any particular church, Mrs. Benton?"

She shrugged. "Used to back home, but not here."

"Then you won't mind if I contact some ministers I know up here and ask if they'll look in on you now and then?"

"I'd be obliged, Pastor Hyde."

"Good! Well, we must be on our way. We've heard some boys up here may know where to find the sheepherder who helped Nate Konning build his barn."

The widow smiled. "Hildy," she began cautiously, "could you leave your coon with my young'uns awhile? They'd be powerful glad, and I'd see they treated the little critter right. We'll be extry keerful of her sore spot."

When Hildy hesitated, Mrs. Benton added, "It's gonna be too hot in the car fer the little critter if ye leave her awhile. An' if ye take her with ye a-walkin', she'll boil in the sun, seein' as how she ain't got no hat like you folks do."

Hildy smiled at the thought of Mischief with a hat. If the little animal rode on Hildy's neck as usual, the girl couldn't wear her hat, either. Hildy didn't like leaving Mischief, but the widow was right. Mischief would be better off with the loving children than in the baking car interior or riding on Hildy's neck in the hot sun.

She nodded. "I suppose it'd be all right to leave her. We could pick her up later today."

The little girls squealed happily, and Mischief was left behind.

Pastor Hyde drove his young friends on through the hot, barren, treeless area. They had no trouble finding the small stream where Brother Kensington said the boys were panning out gold flakes. It was close to Crane's Crossing on the Tres Piedras River to the south.

A distant booming sound meant the dam builders were again blasting away part of a mountainside with dynamite.

Following Brother Kensington's directions, the minister soon found the boys knee deep in a small creek just below some ripples and a slight curve. Gold panning was supposed to be more productive at such places.

Parking the car, Pastor Hyde led Hildy and her friends down to the creek. The boys rose from their crouched positions, their frying pans half-filled with dirt and gravel. Their tattered pants were rolled up to their knees, but they were wet to their elbows from the slow, tedious work.

The minister stopped on the bank. "Finding any color?"

The taller boy answered cautiously. "Got two-dollars-and-two-bits' worth in the last couple days. Almost enough to buy a pair of shoes for one of us. We're trying to git enough today for another pair."

"I trust you'll do that, boys," the pastor said. Then he changed the subject. "My young friends here are looking for someone. A member of our church saw you boys a couple days ago and said you know the whereabouts of two men. One's a sheepherder. The other might be the one for whom we're searching." He turned to Hildy's cousin. "Ruby, please show the boys your snapshot."

Ruby produced the picture from her bib overall pocket and held it out for the boys. They studied it carefully, then exchanged glances.

The shorter boy wiped his hands on his dirty overalls. "This looks sorta like one of them we saw, but it's hard to say for sure."

Ruby put the picture away. "Do ye know whereabouts we kin find him?"

Both boys shook their heads.

"No," the taller boy said, "but the other one's got a camp not far from here."

"Whar?" Ruby asked eagerly.

The taller boy pointed south along the western front of Thunder Mountain. "If you drive down the road beyond that next hill, just past it there's a gully," he said. "Full of water in the winter, but it's dry now. Walk west to where the gully ends in a little valley. The camp's there. You can't miss it."

"Watch out for rattlers, though," the other boy added.

Hildy wished he hadn't said that.

A few minutes later the Chevrolet eased down the dirt road. The hot, dry hills occasionally broke into small cliffs twenty to thirty feet high, paralleling the road on the right.

Spud leaned forward and pointed. "Look at all the holes in those cliffs! And what're those little animals running every-where?"

"Ground squirrels," the pastor replied. "Is this the first time a New York boy like you ever saw any?"

"I've seen prairie dogs, but not ground squirrels," Spud replied. The little rodents gave sharp, whistling alarm calls and scurried for their holes.

Spud laughed at them, then began studying the surrounding area. "Looks like those cliffs where they live was once part of a river," he said. "See how the face is gouged out? Couldn't the stream have undercut the banks and left those cave-like places back underneath?"

The pastor shrugged. "I'm not much on geology, but it could be. After all, this land's been here a mighty long time. Look at Thunder Mountain. It's the highest place around here, yet I understand it was once the lowest."

Hildy looked up at the massive mountain rising on the left. It still seemed dark and threatening, even in full sunlight.

Ruby sat up suddenly in the backseat and pointed. "What's a-hangin' on them thar fence posts yonder?"

Hildy turned to look. "Whatever it is, there's one on every post as far as I can see down the road."

"Coyotes," Pastor Hyde told them. "Maybe poisoned by ranchers or taken by trappers. The carcasses are hung there to show other stockmen that somebody's protecting their calves."

Spud turned around to look at the girls in the backseat. "I heard that coyotes are often unjustly blamed by stockmen. Coy-otes take lambs and maybe a grown sheep now and then, but not calves."

"You'd never convince some of the stockmen in my congregation of that," the preacher replied with a smile.

A few moments later, he began slowing the car. "Well, according to our young friends at the stream," he said, "this must be where we start walking."

He parked at the side of the deserted dirt road, and they helped each other through the barbed wire fence. All four donned hats and eased down into the gully, which rose fifty feet or so on both sides. There were small rocks and gravel in the lowest part where water flowed in winter.

The pastor led and Spud brought up the rear with Ruby and Hildy in between. Hildy looked around anxiously. "Wish we had a stick or something," she said, "in case we see any snakes."

The pastor turned around. "If they hear us coming, they'll probably get out of the way," he said. "Just don't step over any large rocks or put your hands anywhere that a rattler might be sunning itself."

The four walked noisily, scuffing their feet and talking loudly. There was no shade in the middle of the gully, but that was considered the safest course because rattlers would more likely rest along the gully walls.

As the July sun beat down fiercely, Hildy kept her eyes to the ground. Small, wiry plants slapped her shoes. "What's this plant?" she asked. "Is that what I smell?"

"It's tar weed," the minister answered. "It'll make your shoes and everything it touches smelly. Turns pants legs black, too."

"It stinks," Ruby said bluntly. "Or is that somethin' else I'm a-smellin'?"

"Sheep, I bet," Spud said. "I've heard they smell awful."

"We must be getting close," Hildy said. "I think I *hear* sheep now, too."

Ruby, following the minister, reached behind her and gripped her cousin's hand. "Ye reckon that thar sheepherder knows where my daddy is?"

"Let's hope so," Hildy said.

Suddenly Spud called out in a low, urgent voice. "Don't look now," he warned, "but we're being followed!"

CHAPTER THIRTEEN

RETURN TO SIMPLE JUSTICE

H ildy's heart beat faster, but she resisted turning around to
see who was following.

Must be Ozzie Kessick! she thought. *Or his nephew. We're defenseless out here in the open, miles from help—*

Ruby swung around to look. "Man a-horseback," she cautioned. "Jist went down yonder behind that little hill. Got a
rifle."

Hildy's heart leaped. They all could be in danger! She
couldn't stand not knowing who was following them in this
desolate, hilly land.

Stopping in the gully, she turned and waited, staring over
the top of the little cliff to the north at the barren hill beyond.
After a moment, she saw the top of his head. "It's not Mr. Kessick's hat," she said. A second later, the rider came in full view.
"Nobody we know."

Ruby spoke in a low voice. "Might be one o' them night
riders that burned my daddy's barn."

"This man's not wearing a mask," Spud observed. "Oh, he's

turned this way. Now we'll find out who he is."

The stranger, mounted on a chestnut gelding, rode toward them. A heavy hexagon-shaped rifle barrel rested across the saddle horn. His face was shaded by the curled brim of his Columbia-style black hat that had seen years of hard use.

The round tag from a Bull Durham tobacco sack hung from the left breast pocket of his sun-bleached shirt. Hildy knew that meant he smoked "roll-your-own," not "tailor-made" cigarettes.

Laced leather boots with walking heels stuck out from his faded, navy corduroy hiking breeches. Hildy guessed he walked more than he rode.

Ground squirrels sounded their warning whistles and ran for their holes in the gully as the stranger reined his horse and looked down.

"Howdy," he called, easing his stocky body in the saddle with a creaking of leather. "You folks lost?"

Pastor Hyde shook his head. "We're looking for a man, and we heard that maybe the sheepherder in the camp ahead could tell us where to find him."

"You won't learn anything from that herder," the rider said, pointing down the gully. "He's a Basque. Doesn't speak English."

Ruby nudged Hildy. "What's a Basque?" she whispered.

Spud answered quietly, "That's someone from the western Pyrenees in Spain and France. Nobody knows their origin. Their language apparently isn't related to any other."

Hildy shaded her eyes and gazed up at the rider. "The man we're looking for is an American. Tall, slender. You seen him?"

"Sorry, miss. All the herders I know are Basques."

Ruby groaned. "We jist cain't quit now. We gotta find my daddy afore it's too late!"

Spud walked closer to the man. "You live around here?"

"I'm the state lion hunter. On the trail of an outlaw mountain lion. Stock killer. He's been driven out of Thunder Mountain by all the dynamiting. When I get him, he'll be my four hundred eighty-seventh."

Hildy flinched at the idea of anyone killing the big cats. She had never seen one, but she had seen pictures. Still, she understood why cattlemen would want anything dead that might prey on their livestock.

"Mister," Spud said, "can you understand enough of the herder's language to ask if he's seen a man answering the description we've given you?"

The lion hunter smiled. "You'd have as much luck asking as I would. Sorry, folks." He turned the chestnut away. "Well, I got to get back on that outlaw's trail," he said, lifting his left hand in salute.

Suddenly he turned back. "Say, I just remembered. I've heard that there's a new sheepherder southwest of here. Closer to Crane's Crossing. Below Thunder Mountain where it crosses the highest ridge. I've never met him, but I know all the other herders around here are Basques. Whether this new one is or not, you'll have to find out for yourselves."

Again the lion hunter turned his mount away. In moments, he was out of sight behind the hill.

The minister wiped his brow. "Since we're so close, shall we go on down this gully and try talking to the herder? Or shall we turn back and try to locate that new one the lion hunter mentioned?"

Ruby answered without hesitation. "Let's find that new herder. He might be my daddy!"

Hildy looked down the gully. "It's not much farther," she said. "Why don't we try talking to this herder first?"

Spud and the minister agreed. Ruby grumbled with impatience but joined the others as they made their way to the end of the gully.

Hildy surveyed the open, rolling hills beyond. In the distance, a few valley, scrub, and blue oaks grew. A couple of digger pines with wispy branches clung to the highest hill. The grass was knee high and yellowish brown from the scorching sun. With the temperature certainly over a hundred, maybe a hundred and ten, Hildy was glad she had left Mischief with the Bentons.

On the side of the hill thousands of sheep moved over the

ground like an irregular block of grayish white. Several medium-sized dogs dashed around the edges of the flock. They obeyed sharp, brief whistles from a man standing to one side of the mass of sheep. The dogs were mostly black with white collars and chests, but as they drew closer, Hildy noticed that two of the dogs were almost blue with pale blue-black spots.

One of the blue-spotted dogs spotted the visitors. He stopped suddenly, right forefoot high like a bird dog on point. Then he gave a single sharp bark and charged toward Hildy and her friends.

The other dogs followed but stopped on a sharp whistle command from the herder. On a second whistle all the dogs except the closest turned back to their charges. The near dog raced toward the visitors without barking, but also without fear.

"Stand still," Spud told the others. "Don't make any sudden moves."

Everyone stopped, but the dog still charged, running flat out, head extended, straight for the visitors.

Hildy held her breath.

The herder again whistled sharply. Instantly, the dog dropped to the ground a short distance from Hildy. His chin lay on the ground, his ears cocked and alert. He did not move as he watched the visitors approach.

Hildy had never seen a dog that didn't have brown eyes, but this dog's were a strange blend of blue. There was a white circle around the iris of the right eye.

The short, swarthy man moved steadily but unhurried toward his visitors. Wearing an ancient hat, old shirt, pants, and heavy shoes, he carried no staff, which surprised Hildy. He sported a fierce black mustache that flared away from his upper lip in both directions. It looked like some kind of primitive birds trying to escape by flight.

Hildy gulped and looked away from the herder. The area around them was totally desolate. The only sign of a dwelling was a small covered wagon. Its wooden wheels had been blocked so the vehicle wouldn't move. A half-grown bluish dog, tied to the wagon tongue, walked slowly out from under the wagon's shade.

A black stovepipe stuck out on the right rear side of a sun-bleached canvas wagon cover. Below that, the wooden sides looked weathered and gray. On the three-foot-tall sides, six animal hides of various sizes had been stretched and nailed to dry.

The minister seemed to know what Hildy was looking at. "The smaller hides are jackrabbits or cottontails, I think," he said. "Probably uses them to line things because the fur's so soft. The three long hides are coyotes. The middle-sized one must be a bobcat."

Hildy didn't know if the curing hides or the sheep made the terrible smell, but she could hardly keep from being sick.

Spud was still looking at the alert dog guarding the approach to the camp. "I've never seen a dog like this one," he said. "Maybe Australian shepherd. Maybe a Blue Merle. See those blue eyes?"

Hildy wasn't eager to see the dog much closer. She was glad when the herder passed the dog and stopped in front of them.

The man's black eyes bored into the visitors with a fierceness that matched his long mustache. But then, Hildy guessed, a solitary man far from help, defending thousands of sheep against all kinds of enemies, had to be self-reliant.

The minister cleared his throat and extended his hand. "I'm Pastor Hyde," he began. "And these are my young friends—Hildy, Ruby, and Spud. And you are. . . ?

The herder briefly shook the outstretched preacher's hand but said nothing. He looked at the three kids but his black eyes hid his thoughts.

An awkward silence began to build.

"Ruby, show him your picture," the pastor suggested.

Ruby produced the snapshot from her overall bib. "Have ye seen this here man?" she asked, holding the picture close to the herder.

The man took the old photograph in a work-hardened hand and stared at it.

Hildy's hopes rose. "Where can we find him?" she asked loudly, the way people often speak when trying to communicate with someone who doesn't understand their language.

The herder frowned and brought the picture closer to his swarthy face. Cocking his head slightly, he squinted at the picture with one eye half closed.

Spud tried to interpret the man's actions. "I think he may be unsure, but maybe he has seen—"

"Seempleyustis," the herder interrupted.

"What?" the minister asked. "I didn't understand you."

The herder repeated himself, waving the picture to the northeast.

The four looked at each other to see if any had understood. But they all shook their heads.

"Seempleyustis!" the herder repeated louder, imitating Hildy's efforts to communicate better.

Suddenly she understood. "I think he's trying to say *Simple Justice*."

The herder bobbed his head vigorously and smiled, the great black mustache jerking sharply upward. He handed the snapshot back to Ruby.

She tucked it in her overall bib. "What're we a-waitin' fer? Let's go look in Simple Justice agin."

Hildy frowned. "Uh . . . have you forgotten that's where we had trouble with Ozzie Kessick and his nephew?"

"I'm not fergittin' nothin'! I been a-wantin' to meet up with them two polecats agin. I thought all along they knowed whar my pa is, and they done set us off on a wild goose chase."

Ruby turned to the herder and grabbed his hand in a heartfelt handshake. "Much obliged, Mister Sheepherder!" She turned to the others. "Y'all a-comin'? I'm a-gonna find my daddy!"

Waving goodbye to the herder, they all headed back to the car. Hildy was excited for her cousin, but there were practical questions to be asked. "What now? Shall we check out that new herder the lion hunter told us about near Crane's Crossing? Or shall we head for Simple Justice? They're in opposite directions."

"I'm all fer headin' to Simple Justice," Ruby replied.

Spud disagreed. "As long as we're so close to Crane's Crossing, why not check out that new herder?"

Ruby snapped at him. "It don't make no never mind to ye, but I'm a-tryin' to find my daddy! That sheepherder pointed to Simple Justice, and that's whar I'm a-goin'."

"We think that herder said Simple Justice, but we're not sure," he snapped back.

Ruby whirled in the gully to face Spud. "He pointed that-a-way!" she argued.

Spud's face flushed red. "But the lion hunter said—"

"Stop it, you two!" Hildy shouted. "Please."

The minister put his hand on her shoulder. "Since we're so close, why don't we try to find that herder the lion hunter told us about? It shouldn't take too long. If we don't find our man, we could pick up Hildy's raccoon, drive to Simple Justice to ask around, and still get home before dark."

Ruby reluctantly agreed, and the foursome safely traveled the gully again without disturbing any rattlesnakes.

After opening all the doors to briefly air out the Chevrolet's hot interior, they headed south along the glowering black bulk of Thunder Mountain. Before they reached their looked-for landmarks, a man with a red flag waved them to stop.

Through the dust that rose from the unpaved road, the man leaned into the driver's side. "Sorry, folks, but they're dynamiting up ahead. You'll have a couple hours' wait."

It took only a moment for the disappointed driver and passengers to decide they wouldn't wait. The minister turned the car around and headed back. Stopping at the widow's place to reclaim Mischief, they drove on to the old ghost town of Simple Justice.

Entering the town gave Hildy a strange, uneasy feeling. She looked in thoughtful silence as the car eased past the spot where she had helped the drunken sheepherder retrieve his hat from the tormenting boys.

Ruby pointed in the direction Hildy was looking. "Right yonder's whar Hildy an' me stood in the shade of that old buildin' and talked to Ozzie Kessick and his no-count nephew," she said. "If'n I'd a-knowed then what I do now—"

"Look!" Hildy interrupted. "There's Mr. Kessick!"

Ruby yelped. "Stop the car. Please, Pastor Hyde?"

He did, but Ruby jumped out of the backseat before the sedan had come to a complete stop.

"Hey, you!" Ruby called, running down the street. "Wait up!"

Hildy groaned. "She's going to make trouble," she told the minister. "I'll see if I can stop her."

Sprinting from the car, Hildy raced across the street and up on to the high board walk. She was vaguely aware of Spud and Pastor Hyde following at a more leisurely pace.

Ruby stood before Ozzie Kessick, hands on hips, eyes blazing. "Ye done lied to me!" she cried. "Ye and yore nephew sent Hildy and me off a-chasin' after somebody ye knowed was daid! But we didn't quit. Nosireee! Now ye better tell me quick. Whar's my daddy?"

The rancher didn't move. "Young lady," he said coolly, "I suppose we may have met sometime, but—"

"Ye called him Slim," Ruby interrupted, digging into her overall bib pocket, "but he's really this man." She shoved the old snapshot in front of the rancher's nose.

Hildy was close enough to see his eyes flicker with recognition. But he shook his head. "Now I remember you two girls. But I told you then—"

"Jist tell me whar he is," Ruby shrieked, "or so help me, I'll snatch ye bald-headed this very instant!"

Hildy caught up with her cousin and reached out a restraining hand. Ruby was trembling with anger.

Surprisingly, the rancher shrugged and managed a little smile. "Oh, all right. No harm in telling you now. Time is on my side."

He reached into his pocket and removed his round can of snuff. "I wanted that piece of land because it saves two days or more of cattle driving time to and from new range. This tall man you claim is your father wanted to borrow some money to make improvements there. So I loaned—"

"Ye took a mortgage on his land!" Ruby cried. "Ye took it a-purpose, knowin' he prob'ly couldn't pay it back and ye'd foreclose. Ain't that right?"

Hildy wanted to interrupt, but the rancher's cool behavior made her hesitate.

"It's just good business to have collateral, young lady. That's why the mortgage was taken out. So far he hasn't made any payments on that loan. So, unless the mortgage is paid in full by August tenth, that land is mine—all nice and legal."

"Ye cain't do that!" Ruby shouted.

"Why can't I?"

"I got a rich friend! He'll put up the money so's the mortgage is paid on time, even if'n we cain't find my daddy by then."

Hildy was sure Ruby referred to Brother Ben Strong, although Hildy had never heard the possibility of a loan mentioned.

Ozzie Kessick looked Ruby squarely in the eye and spoke quietly and confidentially. "That won't work."

"Shore, it will!" she cried.

"No, it won't. You see, my hot-headed young friend, the agreement specifically states that unless the person who owes the money pays it in person, on time—" Kessick stopped, letting the meaning sink in.

"Go on," Ruby said, but her voice had dropped as though she suspected he was about to say something terrible.

Hildy's mouth suddenly went dry with unnamed fear as she watched her cousin battle this out with the rancher.

"Unless the mortgage is paid on time and *in person* by the one who owes it," Kessick repeated, "the property immediately and legally becomes . . . mine."

CHAPTER FOURTEEN

—

WHEN HOPE IS GONE

Back in the minister's black sedan, Ruby sat quietly, her arms folded across her chest. "Pastor Hyde," she said after they had been riding awhile, "kin a body do that? I mean, put it in writing that the feller who borrowed money has got to repay it personal?"

The pastor glanced at Hildy and Ruby in the rearview mirror. "I'm no expert on contracts, but I suppose that anything the parties agree upon is binding as long as it doesn't break the law."

"So air ye a-sayin' that the mortgage my daddy owes has got to be paid back jist like that o'nry Ozzie Kessick said?"

"Yes, assuming he told you the whole truth."

Ruby leaned forward, disturbing Mischief, who was asleep on the seat between the two girls. "What d'ye mean?"

"Well, Ruby, it's highly unusual, so I am inclined to want to know more."

Spud turned around to face her. "I think what Brother Hyde is trying to say in a tactful way is that we shouldn't accept Kessick's word for what he just told you, Ruby."

Hildy leaned against the seat in front of her. "How could we check on it?"

"First," Spud said, "I think we should take another look at the mortgage and any other papers involved."

"That's a good idea!" Hildy exclaimed. "Brother Hyde, do we have time to swing by the courthouse before going back to the valley?"

The minister glanced back at Hildy and her cousin. "From the look on Ruby's face, I'd say we'd better," he replied.

Spud again volunteered to stay outside with the raccoon while the others went into the courthouse. Reading legal documents was difficult; but together, Hildy, Ruby, and the pastor reviewed the terms of the note signed by Nathaniel Konning and Ozzell Kessick.

Finally, the minister sat up straight and tapped the court record. "There it is, Ruby," he said. "The person signing the note has agreed, as a part of the conditions, to personally repay the note in full by four-fifty-nine o'clock on August tenth."

Ruby's slumped in her chair, but Hildy suddenly gasped and pointed to the page. "Look! There's something else in the fine print."

The others focused their attention where Hildy was pointing. Out loud she read the words *or his heirs*.

"What's that mean?" Ruby asked.

Hildy's voice rose excitedly. "Kin folk," she replied. "An heir is a person like a daughter to her father. Ruby, don't you see what this means? You're his heir, so you could make that payment!"

"Yeah!" Ruby's face broke into a smile. But it immediately faded. "Whar'd I git money to do that?"

Hildy put her hand on her cousin's shoulder. "You mentioned Brother Ben might loan it. Remember?"

"I was jist mouthin' off, Hildy. I cain't ask him fer money."

The pastor frowned. "Girls, there's something about this clause that makes me uneasy."

"How so?" Hildy asked.

"Well, why would such an unusual clause even be considered, let alone put in a document like this?"

"That's easy," Ruby scoffed. "I don't reckon my daddy knows about me."

"That's right!" Hildy exclaimed. "Uncle Nate probably doesn't have any idea that he has a daughter."

The pastor nodded. "That's exactly my point. When that was signed, neither Mr. Kessick nor Mr. Konning knew there was an heir. However, Mr. Kessick does know now, and that might jeopardize his plans for the ranch."

Ruby frowned. "What d'ye mean?"

"Don't you see?" Hildy faced her cousin. "If your father can't make that payment, you can. Even if you don't have the money, Mr. Kessick may think you do. He obviously doesn't want that loan repaid. He wants your father's ranch!"

Ruby's eyes widened. "Reckon that'd 'splain how come that ol' polecat and his nephew acted so strange when I told them who I was and why I was a-lookin' fer—"

"Oh, Ruby!" Hildy interrupted. "Of course! The whole thing makes sense now. That's why Kessick sent us off on a wild goose chase. That's why he lied to you back there a few minutes ago—to make you give up on this whole search."

"There's something else," the pastor said softly. "Ruby's showing up unexpectedly might put her in danger. Maybe her father and you, too, Hildy."

Considerably sobered by the possibilities, the cousins and the minister returned to Spud and the raccoon. Getting back into the car, they told Spud what they found at the courthouse.

"That does seem to place you both in jeopardy," he agreed.

As they rolled past a general store on the way through town, the pastor pointed off to the right. "Look," he said, "there's Mr. Kessick again. See? Loading up that spring wagon in front of the store."

"An' his no 'count nephew, too," Ruby grumbled. "Looks like they got a passel of staples there. They must have a mighty big family."

The pastor shook his head. "More likely they're taking supplies out to one of their ranches."

Spud turned to watch the Kessicks as the car passed them. "Why wouldn't they use a truck instead of a wagon?"

Hildy glared at them through the back window. "Maybe because where they're going it's too rough for a truck?"

"Whar might that be?" Ruby asked.

Hildy and Spud looked at each other; then Hildy turned back

to her cousin. "Maybe a sheep camp?"

Ruby cocked her head thoughtfully. "You mean, maybe he knows whar my daddy is, and he's a-takin' them thar vittles—?"

"There's one way to find out," Spud said. "They're just pulling away from the curb. Pastor Hyde, do you think we could stop a minute at that store and ask some questions?"

"Good idea," the pastor replied. "I'm thirsty. Let's turn around and go back. I'll treat all of us to a Nehi soda."

The four of them walked into the store past stacked gunny sacks of barley and some salt licks for stock. Inside, the store was packed with countless items that rested on high shelves, hung from overhead racks, or were packed helter-skelter along the wooden floor.

"Afternoon, folks," the proprietor said from behind the crowded counter. He was a short, skinny man with butcher paper taped to his forearms to protect his sleeves. "Hot enough for you?"

"Shore is," Ruby said, wiping her brow with the back of her hand. "We need us a sody pop."

"Help yourselves in the box behind you," the man offered.

Hildy watched the pastor as he removed each bottle from the water-filled box with floating chunks of ice. Yanking off the caps for the young people, he handed out the sodas and everyone took a sip.

Hildy smiled at the skinny storeowner. "You seem to have about everything under the sun."

"General mercantile," the merchant replied proudly, dusting tops of cans with an ancient feather duster. "Try to please the folks that live hereabouts."

Spud looked into a cracker barrel that stood open on the floor. "I guess your main trade is with ranchers?"

"Mostly, yes. A few people like you folks stop by now and again. Sometimes a sheepherder comes in town and buys a few things. But they're not too popular around here. People say sheep smell, but I say cattle do, too."

Hildy laughed. "Come to think of it, they sure do."

"Depends on what you're used to," the proprietor said, re-arranging some canned goods on a shelf. "Until recently, no self-respecting cattleman would run sheep. But I have a customer—

he was in here not five minutes ago—and he recently started buying sheep, running both them and cattle."

The four visitors exchanged startled glances.

Shaking his head, the skinny man said, "I never thought I'd see the day. But then, I guess the name of the game is to make money. And if you can make that by running both sheep and cattle, then I guess that's the right thing to do. At least in Mr. Kessick's case."

"Mr. Kessick?" Hildy repeated, lowering her strawberry soda.

"Fellow I was telling you about. Comes in here regular, once a week, loads his wagon and takes it out to some sheep ranch. 'Course, he doesn't say that's what he's doing, but I know that's what it is."

Spud leaned against the counter. "How can you tell that?"

"Well, he just bought some stovepipe. Two three-foot sections. That's not enough for any cowboy's bunkhouse, but it's enough for a sheepherder's wagon."

Hildy nodded, remembering the stovepipe she had seen sticking out of the Basque's covered wagon.

"Whar'bouts is this here sheep ranch?" Ruby asked.

"Don't rightly know. Southwest of here, I'd guess, because that's the only back country that's too rough for a truck. Have to use a team and wagon."

Spud casually took a drink of his grape soda. "You say that man comes in here regularly for supplies?"

"Be back a week from today. You can count on it."

When they returned to the car, Hildy nearly burst with this new information. "If we could come back then, and had more time, we could follow Mr. Kessick and find that sheep ranch," she said.

"I cain't wait no week!" Ruby wailed. "Ever' day is takin' my daddy closer to rack and ruin."

Pastor Hyde shook his head and started the car. "I'm sorry. I can't take you three again for a while, either," he said, heading out of town. "I have a very busy schedule."

Ruby curled up in the backseat and stifled a sob.

Hildy reached over and touched her cousin's arm. "It'll be all right," she said.

Ruby's chin quivered. "I jist cain't stand it, Hildy. After all these years a-not knowin' if'n I had a real daddy er not, and then to find out he's close by but not bein' able to find hide ner hair of him—"

"We'll find him," Hildy whispered with conviction. "Brother Ben said he'd help, and Pastor Hyde and Spud are helping."

"I know, but time's 'bout gone," she wailed in despair, "and we ain't comin' no closer to findin' him."

"Don't give up, Ruby. Please? You've got to believe it's going to work out."

"Believe?" Ruby said the word as though tasting it. "It gets powerful hard to believe when nothin's goin' right."

Hildy silently prayed that she would be able to say something to help her cousin. "Sometimes," she began uncertainly, "belief or faith is all we've got, but that's powerful! Think about it. When you and I set out from the Ozarks to find Molly and the kids, we had nothing except the belief we'd find them."

Ruby sniffed and managed a little smile. "Yore fergittin' we also had us a couple tow sacks with ever'thing we owned in 'em."

Hildy returned the smile. "You know what I mean. We set out alone—"

"Dressed up like boys!"

Hildy nodded. "And we kept going across country with just the desire to find my family." She paused. "We found Molly and the kids, and now we're a family again. Someday, I know we're going to find our 'forever' home where we won't have to move again."

The minister glanced back at them. "There's a verse in Proverbs about that. It says, 'As he thinketh in his heart, so is he.' Your beliefs govern your life, and belief in God is the most powerful of all."

"I jist want to find my daddy," Ruby replied.

"Then you've got to believe you're going to," Hildy said emphatically. "I believe it."

Ruby lapsed into silence, and no one else said anything until the Chevrolet slowed and turned into the Corrigan driveway.

Spud sat up suddenly. "Uh-oh!" he exclaimed. "Trouble!"

CHAPTER
FIFTEEN

———

MYSTERIOUS DISAPPEARANCES

Not far from the barn-house a heavy-set, uniformed deputy sheriff stood next to his patrol car talking to Hildy's stepmother. Molly held the baby across her left hip while all four of Hildy's little sisters clustered around their stepmother's skirt.

Scooping up Mischief, Hildy leaped out of the backseat as soon as Pastor Hyde stopped the car. She ran up to Molly and the others. "What's the matter? Is Daddy—?"

"It's all right, Hildy," Molly said. "This officer was checking on a neighbor's complaint about your raccoon."

Anger surged through Hildy. "You mean the Jarmans!"

The deputy tipped his hat. "This the coon they complained about?"

Molly nodded. "As you can see, Mischief couldn't be responsible for the Jarmans' troubles. She's been with Hildy all day up in the foothills."

As the pastor, Ruby, and Spud joined them, the minister extended his hand. "I'm Pastor Hyde," he said, "and I can vouch for the fact that this animal was with us all day."

The deputy shook the pastor's hand. "I'll report to the Jarmans. But from what you've told me, Mrs. Corrigan, I don't think that's going to satisfy them."

Hildy clutched her raccoon tighter. "They're just doing those things to make me trade Mischief to them!" she cried. "I won't do that. They'd let their dogs chase her and probably kill her!"

The deputy apologized but said there was nothing more he could do. Getting into his patrol car, he drove away.

The pastor left shortly after that to get ready for prayer meeting. Then Hildy, Ruby, and Spud went inside the barn-house to tell Molly and the little girls what had happened in the foothills that day.

After Hildy and her companions related the main details, Hildy's sisters took the raccoon outside to play. Molly put Joey down for a nap, then joined the others around the kitchen table.

Ruby sighed loudly. "Tomorry'll be a full week gone by." She twisted around to count the days on the calendar hanging by the kitchen range. "That jist leaves thirteen days this month and nine the next."

"Ten," Hildy corrected. "August tenth would be ten more days."

"I'm not a-countin' that day," Ruby argued, "'cause it's the one when the money's due. If'n it ain't paid by then, Daddy loses his ranch!"

"Not until five o'clock that afternoon," Hildy reminded her. "So we've really got twenty-three days—better than three weeks."

Ruby pouted. "Don't matter none 'cause nobody's a-goin' back up to them hills for who knows how long. Cain't find my daddy a-sittin' here."

She paused, then brightened. "Hey! I got me a idee. I'm a-gonna go up there myself an' look around till I find him."

Molly protested. "Oh, my, Ruby! You can't do that!"

"Why not?" she demanded, jumping up. "Hildy and I set out from the Ozarks by ourselves, and we made it."

"With the good Lord's help," Molly said. "But I'm not going to let Hildy go with you, and you certainly can't do that alone."

Spud pounded his fist on the table. "Molly's right. It's too dangerous."

"Ye keep out of this!" Ruby snapped. "It ain't none of yore business."

A flush of anger washed over Spud's face. Before he could answer, Hildy reprimanded her cousin. "Don't talk to Spud that way," she said. "He cares what happens to you, Ruby."

"Shore he does," Ruby replied sarcastically.

"Well, I do," Spud said in a tight voice, "whether you believe it or not, Ruby Konning."

Ruby thought for a moment, then shrugged. "I thankee, but if'n I cain't find my daddy, then what good is it fer me to go on a-livin?"

"Ruby!" Hildy jumped up and threw her arms around her cousin. "Don't ever say anything like that! Not ever!"

Ruby's body was tense. "I was a-readin' in one a them thar women's magazines somebody give Molly all about what kids need . . ." she said.

". . . like secur'ty, playin', lovin' an' bein' loved, knowin', an' all sech things. Well, I ain't got no secur'ty. I'm a-livin' with some folks who're givin' me a place to sleep an' eat 'cause they're nice people. But I don't belong to nobody er nothin'.'"

"Yes, you do," Molly argued. "You're a part of our family."

"I thankee fer sayin' that, Molly, but that ain't the same as havin' my own family. Got me no sisters ner brothers. Got no mother. I jist found out I got me a daddy, but what good's it a-doin' me if'n I cain't find 'im?"

"You'll find him!" Hildy said. "I've told you over and over—"

Ruby interrupted as though she hadn't heard. "Ain't never done much. Ain't hardly edycated. Don't know much, neither. Ain't never really played in my whole life," she complained. "Mosta the time when I was growin' up I was fightin' somebody fer sayin' somethin' mean an' nasty about my mother or about me not havin' no daddy."

Molly looked at the girl with concern. "Ruby, you've been fighting the world for a long time, and it's not fair for one young lady to have to take on so much. But it'll work out all right. You'll see."

Ruby looked around the room. "Y'all got secur'ty—well, no money to speak of—but ye got each other. Uncle Joe's got him a job when millions o' men cain't find work. Ye got this barn-house. Ye belong to the church and people come visit ye 'cause they care. Yore a lovin' family—ye even love that thar coon!"

"We love you, too," Hildy assured her.

Ruby droned on, her voice sounding sadder with each comment. "Y'all air gonna achieve somethin'. That's the word it used in the magazine. Yore all a-gonna have a 'forever' home and ye know that. An' the kids play. I kin hear 'em outside, playin' all the time."

She turned, fighting back tears. "An' look at the decorations ye got," she said. "Even in this barn, ye got pi'tchers cut outta magazines and stuck up around the walls to make it purdy. But me—I got nothin'. Ain't never gonna have nothin', neither."

Spud leaned forward. "What about me?"

Ruby's temper flared. "Ye got a home and family! But ye done run off-a yore own accord. Ye at least got somethin' if'n ye want it. I want somethin' I ain't got, and I cain't have it." She whirled and ran out the sliding barn door.

Hildy started to follow, but Molly restrained her. "Let her go," she urged. "Ruby needs some time to be alone. We'd better watch to see that she doesn't take off, though."

———

On Saturday night, a pickup truck dropped Joe Corrigan off in front of the barn-house, and the whole family ran out to meet him.

Elizabeth gave her dad a hug and kiss, then asked, "Where's your car, Daddy?"

Joe Corrigan took the baby from Molly and put his arm around his wife's waist. "You won't believe this," he answered, "but it got smashed."

"Oh, Joe!" Molly exclaimed. "An accident? Are you hurt?"

"I'm fine. In fact, I wasn't even in the car when it happened. Come inside and I'll tell you all about it."

When they were all seated around the kitchen table, Joe Corrigan began his explanation. "You all know I stayed in the ranch bunkhouse this week while we unloaded all those wild Nevada cows and drove them to different ranges. Well, this afternoon the boss let us off early. I decided that I'd drive home by way of the dam and see how it's coming."

"Oh, Joe," Molly whispered. "You didn't get close to where they're dynamiting?"

"I parked the Lexington and climbed up on a hill where I could see better," he continued. "Guess I overlooked the red flags down below."

"Red flags?" Elizabeth asked.

"They mean that there's going to be an explosion, and everybody should keep away," Hildy explained.

"But you didn't see them?" Martha prompted.

"'Fraid not," he replied. "Anyway, while I was standing on this hill, looking down at the dam, all of a sudden I heard someone shout, 'Fire in the hole!' "

He turned to Elizabeth. "That means that a fuse is burning, and dynamite's going to explode."

"What about the car?" Elizabeth persisted.

"I was coming to that." He took a deep breath. "Well, right after the warning, a bunch of whistles blew, and the whole mountain seemed to jump. Almost knocked me off my feet. Well, when I got back down to where I'd left the car, it was gone."

"Gone?" everyone asked together.

"Buried under all the rocks and dirt that slid down the mountainside from the dynamite explosion."

"Oh, Daddy!" Hildy exclaimed. "Thank the Lord you're safe!" But she couldn't help but feel sad about their Lexington Minuteman. She remembered how they had found such a good deal on it in Illinois, and how it brought them safely to California.

Molly hugged her husband. "Yes, thank the Lord you weren't hurt!" She paused. "But what're you going to do about another car?" she asked.

Joe Corrigan sighed. "We got no money for one, so I'll just have to see if I can trade something."

Hildy leaned forward. "Maybe Brother Strong'd have some

ideas," she suggested. "Could we invite him to eat with us after church tomorrow?"

"We don't have a thing in the house except beans and potatoes," Molly objected.

"But couldn't we ask him anyway?"

Molly agreed, so the next day, between Sunday school and church service, Hildy rushed up to the tall, stately old gentleman and extended the invitation.

When she apologized for the menu, the old ranger smiled. "Beans and potatoes are my favorites," he said. "Tell Molly I'd be proud to come if you can ride with me to your place."

After church, Hildy rode in the front seat of the Packard with the old ranger.

As they rolled toward the Corrigans' barn-house, Brother Strong brought up a painful memory. "Do you remember when that well-to-do woman in the store called your family *Okies*?"

"I'll never forget!"

"You remember I told you that people called me that when I arrived in Lone River?"

When Hildy nodded, the man continued. "That bothered me a lot. I'd been fairly well off in Oklahoma before the dust storms ruined me financially. I drifted to California, dressed in rags, and looked like I didn't have a dime to my name, which I didn't."

Hildy ran her hand over the rich upholstery of the luxury car and listened to the purring of the powerful motor. "Then how'd you go from that to this? What changed?"

"My attitude."

"Your attitude?"

"Yes, Hildy. You see, being an *Okie* or anything else that people look down on is mostly the result of an attitude. I hear it all the time. People say, 'I never had nothin'. Ain't never gonna have nothin'.' And they're right."

Hildy remembered what Ruby had said along those lines.

The ranger continued. "I hear this defeatist attitude everywhere. It's even in music—all sad and melancholy and looking at the dark side of life. That's only reinforcing the wrong things. People ought to listen to what the Bible says about attitude."

"I don't remember that word being in the Bible."

"It's not. But think of what it does say about having faith and not fearing—to trust and watch what you say and think."

"You're right, Brother Ben. I can remember a bunch of them real fast."

"There's one thing that bothered me for a long time," the old ranger admitted. "That's when Jesus taught that whoever has will be given more. And whoever does not have, even what he thinks he has shall be taken from him. Remember?"

"I've read that."

"Jesus repeats that thought five times: once in Mark and twice in both Matthew and Luke. Now, why do you think He did that?"

"To make it plain, I guess."

"Exactly, Hildy. For emphasis. It seems to be a divine principle. Anyway, I made up my mind that I was going to get out of my money troubles. And I did."

"I'm not sure I understand."

"I put God first and trusted that I had what it took to achieve things. With my changed attitude, many other things changed. People quit calling me *Okie*. Now they call me sir."

Something clicked in Hildy's memory. "As a man thinks in his heart, so is he," she quoted.

"Right. So watch your thoughts, Hildy. For whatever you think is going to show up just as surely as when you plant tomatoes you're going to get more tomatoes—not corn."

Hildy leaned forward in the seat as the Packard slowed for the turn into the lane leading to the barn-house. *Was it the difference between her and Ruby's thoughts that made their lives so different?* Hildy wondered.

Brother Strong parked the car, and Hildy's father slid the barn door open for them. Hildy saw by the look on his face that something had happened.

Jumping out of the car, she ran to meet him. "Daddy! Something wrong?"

"The people where Ruby's been staying came by a while ago," he said soberly. "She's disappeared—and so has your coon!"

CHAPTER SIXTEEN

THE SEARCH BEGINS

Hildy frantically pestered her father with questions. He tried to calm her down, but it was the old ranger's quiet voice that reached through Hildy's sudden fear and anguish.

Brother Strong gently touched her hand. "Please, Hildy," he said. "Let me."

Numbly, she nodded, then listened as the old man skillfully asked the questions that most needed answers. By then Molly and the kids had arrived home from church, and they all gathered around to listen.

When Joe Corrigan finished telling them everything he knew about the situation, Brother Ben turned and nodded with satisfaction. "Obviously, Ruby ran away to find her father. At least we know approximately where to begin looking for her," the old ranger said.

He smiled down at his young friend. "As for your little pet, Hildy, she's only been gone a couple of hours. She may just be wandering around in the berry vines or something. So maybe the children could look for Mischief while the rest of us concentrate on what to do about Ruby."

Elizabeth proudly offered to take Martha and search the outbuildings, the blackberry vines, and the pastures. Sarah and Iola agreed to examine the rest of the barn and places close to the house.

When the younger sisters had run off to begin their quest, Hildy and the others sat around the table. Brother Strong sat across from her, and though she was glad the old ranger was with them, she wished Spud were there, too. But she didn't say that aloud.

Brother Ben absently spun the brim of his white hat through his big fingers. "From what you've told me, I don't think Ruby's in any real danger from Ozzie Kessick," he said. "Granted, she is now a threat to his plans to get Nate Konning's ranch. But Kessick only tried to fool her and scare her off. I don't think the stakes are high enough for him to deliberately harm her."

Hildy sighed with relief. "I'm glad of that, but how'll we find her?"

"The obvious place to start is that new sheepherder's camp the lion hunter told you about."

Hildy cringed, thinking of her father's car buried under rocks and dirt. "That's where they're doing all the dynamiting for the dam," she said. "They made us turn back because of the blasting. But that won't stop Ruby if she thinks her father's near there."

"I'm afraid you're right, Hildy," the old ranger agreed.

Joe Corrigan slapped his open palm on the table so hard his baby son let out a frightened cry. Molly comforted the child while Joe explained his action.

"If I had my car—"

"Joe," the old man said gently, "even if you did, you can't afford to take time off work. Your family needs that income. And jobs are too scarce for you to risk losing one unnecessarily. I'll drive up and look for Ruby."

Hildy frowned, remembering something he had told her earlier. "But you're right in the middle of some big land deal, aren't you?" she protested.

"One girl is worth more than any sale I might make."

Hot tears instantly filled Hildy's eyes. "Oh, Brother Ben! If

Ruby could hear you say that—"

He waved her to silence. "If it's okay with your folks, Hildy, I'd like to have you ride along."

Hildy smiled warmly. "Thank you."

Her father cleared his throat and spoke with eyes downcast. "Hildy, you'll need food, and—"

"Don't give that another thought," the old ranger broke in.

Hildy's father looked up. "I'm obliged to you. I'll make it up to you."

"Forget it, Joe! Just pray that we find Ruby."

Joe Corrigan nodded and lowered his eyes again. Hildy wondered if he really would pray. She knew Molly would.

Although eager to get going, Hildy had a suggestion. "Could we drive by Spud's tree house and see if he can go with us?" she asked.

When the old ranger nodded, Molly said, "Tell Spud we'll take care of Lindy. Now, while Hildy gets ready, I'll pack a lunch for all of you."

Hildy quickly gathered the few belongings she might need. Her shoes were in poor shape because of long, hard use. The recent walk with Pastor Hyde to the Basque's sheep camp had torn them up even worse. But since they were all she had except for her Sunday ones, which weren't made for hard walking, she slipped them on and headed for the door.

Molly handed Hildy a silvery lard pail. "It's got fresh biscuits and boiled potatoes to eat along the way," she said.

As Hildy and the old ranger started to leave, all four younger sisters reported back on their search for the missing raccoon.

"No sign of her," Elizabeth said with a hint of tears in her eyes.

Hildy nodded. "That leaves the Jarmans as a possibility." She fought back feelings of anger and resentment toward the coon hunter and his son. "If they hurt Mischief . . ." she muttered through clenched teeth.

Joe Corrigan put his arm around her. "I'll walk over and have a talk with them," he promised.

"Thanks, Daddy." Hildy gave him a quick kiss on the cheek.

"I'll ride back up to the foothills with the foreman tomorrow morning early," he said, giving her a hug. "I'll have to stay at the bunkhouse all week again. But when you find Ruby—"

"We'll come by and let you know," the old ranger assured him.

Joe nodded his thanks. "If you need to stay overnight up there, the boss lets men stay in the bunkhouse a night or two when they're passing through. There are some extra beds. I'm sure you'd be welcome."

"I'll remember," the old ranger replied. "Now, Hildy, if you're ready, let's go get Spud."

As soon as the big yellow-and-black Packard drove into the yard, Spud climbed down from his tree house. After listening to what Hildy and Brother Ben had to say, Spud promptly agreed to help. He coaxed Lindy into the backseat. Then after they delivered the Airedale to the Corrigans', Brother Ben turned the luxury car toward the foothills.

"Please, Lord," Hildy whispered from the backseat, "take care of Ruby."

After they had eaten the lunch Molly had sent along and driven for about an hour, the conversation began to slow down. "Well," the old ranger said, "we've discussed nearly everything we can about Ruby. There's nothing more we can do for her until we get there. And Hildy," he said, glancing in the rearview mirror, "I'm sure Mischief will turn up safe."

Hildy and Spud nodded in agreement, though Hildy couldn't help but worry a little bit.

Finally the old ranger changed the topic. "Hildy, what're your plans when you grow up?"

"I'm planning to get an education," she answered. "Then maybe I'll teach school."

The old man nodded approval. "That's good thinking, Hildy. However, there are lots of men with doctoral degrees—Ph.D's and the like—who can't get work in this Depression. So education alone isn't the answer. It's part of it, but the real secret is in the mind."

Spud turned and leaned back against the passenger door.

"The mind?" he said, looking directly at the driver. "Like Jung and Adler and Freud?"

Hildy squirmed. She had talked of getting an education and considered herself fairly bright, but she had never heard those names.

Ben Strong smiled. "No, not those. I was thinking of One greater than any of those when it comes to understanding the human mind."

"Greater than Sigmund Freud?" Spud asked in surprise. "He's still alive, you know. And he's having a lot of influence on people's thinking. Who's better than he?"

"Oh, I was thinking of a carpenter."

Spud sputtered in indignation. "A carpenter?"

Hildy suddenly understood and didn't feel so left out. "You mean the One from Galilee, Brother Ben?"

"That's the One, Hildy."

Spud glanced sharply at her, then slowly drew back in his seat. "Oh, you're talking religion now."

"Not religion, Spud," the driver said. "Great truths taught in the best psychology book ever written."

Spud had obviously lost interest but remained polite. "Like what?" he asked without enthusiasm.

"Without discussing the spiritual aspects," Brother Ben answered, keeping his eyes on the road, "let's talk about what He did that showed us what we should do."

Hildy leaned forward and put her hands on the back of the front seat. "What do you mean?"

"Well," the old ranger said, "for instance, when He was twelve years old, He showed that He had a purpose in life."

Hildy nodded. "In the temple. Listening to the elders, then telling Joseph and Mary, 'I must be about My Father's business.' "

"Purpose," the driver repeated. "He had a purpose."

Spud sat up. "I looked up the word *purpose* in my dictionary once. It means both the reason for something and the intended result."

"Good," the ranger said. "And next, He had a plan."

Hildy looked up. "Plan?"

"Well, the Bible doesn't use that exact word to describe it," the old ranger conceded; "but remember the story about a man building a tower and a king thinking about going to war against two other kings?"

Hildy nodded. "I see. That meant planning."

"Yes, and there was a plan for this world before it ever was. In fact, there was a plan for everything that carpenter did while He was here."

A few verses flashed through her mind. "Yes, of course. Now that you mention it . . ."

"Finally, He persevered," the old ranger continued.

Hildy thought about all the people who had opposed Him, all the difficulties He had with His own family and disciples, all the pain. "You're right," she agreed. "He never quit. He never gave up."

"Millions of lives around the world have been changed because of Him," Brother Strong said quietly. "And it's not over yet."

"Purpose. Plan. Persevere," Hildy repeated. "Brother Ben, is that what makes some folks achieve more in life than others?"

"Think about it," the old ranger replied.

Spud turned to Hildy. "You're always talking about a 'forever' home. That's your purpose."

"But how am I going to make it happen?" she asked. "What's my plan? Oh, Brother Ben, if you're right, I might have gone on for years talking about getting that place and never really doing it. Now I know I can't ever give up!"

"Lots of good, well-meaning folks daydream, Hildy," the old ranger told her. "They talk about what they want to do. Maybe you could call it a 'fairy godmother complex' or wishful thinking. But only those who go beyond their dreams—those who plan and stick to it—really reach their goals. I want you to reach yours, Hildy. So I hope what I've said will help."

"Oh, it's already helped." Hildy glanced at Spud. "How about you?" she asked.

His green eyes clouded as though he was shutting something

out—maybe her. He did not answer but turned slowly to look out the windshield.

Brother Strong flipped his mustache. "Speaking of plans," he said, "it's about time to put our first one into action. Our turnoff for Thunder Mountain is just up ahead."

Hildy tensed as the Packard crept along the dirt road, throwing up a tail of dust. As they drove along the frowning black mass of ancient volcanic stone, they passed by Mrs. Benton's and soon reached the strange, small cliffs riddled with ground squirrel holes.

Hildy sat forward to look out. "It was just past here that a flagman stopped us when Pastor Hyde was driving," she said. "We had to turn back because they were blasting up ahead."

Spud pointed. "Look beyond that next curve. See? Rising up above the hills, that high point must be the ridge the lion hunter told us about. That herder's camp is supposed to be near there."

Ben Strong peered through the dust-clouded windshield. "We have seen very few trees up till now, but there's a line of them in the distance. They must be growing along the Tres Piedras River, where they're building the dam."

Spud agreed. "The lion hunter said it was between Crane's Crossing and where we met him."

"That's right on the river," the old ranger said. "I've been there a few times. Well, soon's I can find a safe place to pull off and leave the car, we'll walk."

Hildy glanced at the western sky. "Think we can find it before dark?"

"Since we don't know how far it is, we'll just have to start searching," Brother Strong told her. "If it looks as if we can't make it, we'll turn around."

"Maybe we'll have to turn around before then," Spud warned. "Look up ahead."

In a couple of minutes, the Packard braked to a stop in front of flickering road flares and a sign that read: Danger. Road Closed. Explosives in Use.

Hildy groaned. "This is Sunday! How come they're doing that now?"

The old ranger shrugged. "It doesn't matter why. The fact is, we can't go on tonight."

"What'll we do?" Hildy asked. "Turn back and try to find the bunkhouse Daddy told about? Mrs. Benton's got no room, and there's not a tourist cabin anywhere in these foothills that I've seen."

"First," Brother Strong said, "as long as we're passing Mrs. Benton's, I suggest we stop and tell her what happened. Maybe she's heard or seen something that might help us find Ruby. Then let's drive into Shaw's Ferry and try to get something to eat," he said. "After that, we'll see if we can find the ranch your father mentioned. Maybe we can spend the night in the bunkhouse. I'm sure they'd have a place for a girl, too, or your father wouldn't have suggested it."

Hildy and Spud exchanged glances, then nodded. The old ranger turned the car around and headed north. Finally, he slowed the automobile at the barren driveway leading to the sod house at the foot of Thunder Mountain.

Hildy pointed ahead. "They must have heard us coming," she said. "There's Jacob. He must be mighty glad to see us. Look how he's climbing out of there!"

"It's more than that." The old ranger stopped the car. "That boy's flat-out running."

The three jumped out and hurried to meet him.

Jacob's wide eyes showed fear. "Come quick!" he panted as he got close. "Somethin' turrible's happened!"

CHAPTER
SEVENTEEN

—

MISERY AT THE SOD HOUSE

Hildy, Spud, and Ben Strong hurried after Jacob, entering the sod house through a crude, squeaky door. The sod house reminded Hildy of the storm cellar back home. Rickety stairs led down into one large room with a dirt floor and sparse furniture. A single kerosene lamp rested on an upturned wooden packing crate that served as a table.

Hildy's eyes took a moment to adjust to the contrast between the late afternoon sunlight and the dugout's gloominess. The younger children's eyes were filled with fear and the baby whimpered as she clung to one of her sisters.

Jacob, with all the bravery he could muster for his ten years, led the way to a pallet of old blankets in the corner of the musty-smelling room.

"Mama's poorly," he explained. "See?"

Hildy bent over the stricken woman. Mrs. Benton was bare-footed but fully clothed in a frayed, tattered dress. Her glasses lay on the blankets beside her, and her face was pale. Moist strands of her scraggly, uncombed hair clung to her forehead.

Her eyes flickered open. "Ruby?" she whispered.

"No, I'm Hildy. With Spud and Brother Strong. What's wrong?"

"I'm feelin' kinda puny," the widow said in a weak voice. "Been a-comin' on fer some time, but today it seemed to hit kinda sudden-like. I tried to keep a-goin' to he'p my young'uns, but . . . I'm so . . . tired." Her eyes closed.

Hildy turned to Spud and Brother Ben. "What'll we do?" she asked softly.

The widow's children had gathered silently around the visitors. The two-year-old clutched her empty Coca-Cola bottle with the nipple. The child's tiny hand reached up to Hildy's. Hildy gripped it reassuringly.

Jacob looked up at Hildy with pleading eyes. "Is she going to heaven like Papa done?"

Hildy impulsively knelt, released the child's hand, and pulled all four children to her. Out of the corner of her eye, she saw Brother Strong lean over and touch the woman's forehead, then feel her pulse.

Hildy spoke to the children quietly. "We'll need each of you to be brave. Can you do that?"

"I kin!" Jacob said stoutly. A single tear slipped down his dirty cheek, leaving a small trail that glistened in the lamplight.

"Of course you can," Hildy assured him.

Brother Ben released Mrs. Benton's wrist and stood up with a grave expression on his face.

What did that mean? Hildy wondered. She needed to talk to him, but she also wanted to quiet the children's fears. "Let's see," she said, trying to sound cheerful. She looked at each child in turn. "Jacob, you're the only boy, are you the oldest?"

"Yep, I am," he said. "Folks back home said I was the man of the house now that Papa done gone to be with Jesus."

Hildy hugged the boy close. "Oh Jacob! That's such a heavy burden to lay on a ten-year-old! You need to be a boy for a long time yet!"

The moment she said it, Hildy remembered that she hadn't been much older when her own mother died. Hildy had suddenly become mother to her younger sisters and baby brother. Much of that time, her father was away, looking for work. When he married Molly, Hildy didn't have to bear such heavy responsibilities, but she never really had a childhood.

Hildy turned to the oldest girl. "You're Rachel, aren't you?"

The girl nodded solemnly. "I'm seven."

Hildy looked at the next girl. "Rhonda, isn't it? How old are you?"

The girl held up four fingers.

"You're four!" Hildy cried. "And I remember that Becky here is nearly two. Well, you're all very good kids." She looked over at the oldest again. "Jacob, why don't you take the other kids outside for a few minutes while I talk with Brother Ben and Spud about how to help your mother?"

When the children had filed out, Hildy turned anxious eyes on the old ranger.

He sighed heavily. "She's feverish. Pulse very fast. No rash or anything to indicate a disease. But I'd better go see if I can find a doctor." He turned to leave.

Spud started after him. "What can I do?"

Hildy quickly remembered some of the things she had done for her mother when she was so sick. "Ask Rachel or Jacob to find a cloth," she told him. "Then get some cool water and soak the cloth for me, please."

The old ranger headed up the rickety stairs. "I'll be back soon's possible," he promised.

Spud trailed behind him.

Hildy bent over Mrs. Benton, listening to her labored breathing. The dim, underground room suddenly brightened as Brother Ben opened the squeaking door and he and Spud went out. Then it was gloomy again. Hildy turned to the big wooden crate and picked up the lamp, holding it close to see the woman's face more clearly.

Mrs. Benton's eyes opened slowly. "Ruby?" she said in a weak, tired voice.

"No, I'm her cousin, Hildy."

"Ye done good, Ruby, 'cause I didn't think ye'd been gone

long enough to git he'p. I'll . . . be all right . . . soon's I git me
. . . some rest."

Hildy stood up and replaced the lamp, wishing Spud would
hurry with the wet cloth. *Guess she's out of her mind, imagining
Ruby's been here,* she thought. *Wish I knew what was wrong with
her . . . and what we're going to do with these children. . . .* Hildy
remembered the pain of when her own mother had died.

It was late in the day when Ben Strong returned with a country doctor.

The wiry little physician brought with him the customary
black bag and a no-nonsense manner. "Everybody wait outside,
please," he said, "except you." He indicated Hildy with a slight
motion of his right hand.

As Brother Ben and Spud herded the Benton children up the
stairs, Spud whispered to Hildy. "Jacob says Ruby was here
today."

Hildy blinked in surprise. "Then Mrs. Benton wasn't even
imagining—"

"Ruby went looking for a neighbor to help."

Sudden panic gripped Hildy. "That must have been hours
ago!" she exclaimed, trying to keep her voice down.

"She had to walk. I told Brother Ben. We're going to take the
kids and go driving around. Won't take long. There aren't that
many houses where she could have gone."

Late afternoon sunlight flooded the room as the sod house
door squealed open. A moment later, Hildy heard the Packard
pull away. She turned to watch the doctor complete his examination.

At length he stood up and stuck the stethoscope in his
pocket. "You her daughter?"

"No. Sort of a friend. The little ones are her children. Oldest
is ten." Hildy glanced at the woman lying so still. "She going to
be okay?"

"Yes and no," the doctor replied. "She's suffering from se-
vere malnutrition. I suspect she's been giving her kids most of
the food she should have been eating. Primarily, she's just worn
out and too discouraged to keep on."

"You mean . . . she's not sick enough to die, but she might?"

The wiry little doctor nodded. "I see a lot of cases like this. The Depression's getting them down. They have so much misery for so long that they finally give up on living. And they die."

"But . . . Mrs. Benton can't do that," Hildy protested quietly. "Her children—"

"She's too fatigued and discouraged to think logically right now. She needs someone to care for her, to give her a reason for living. Otherwise . . ." He shrugged.

Some time later Hildy heard the Packard pull up outside. Running up the stairs, she pushed open the door. Dusk had fallen, and in the headlights, she saw Spud, Brother Ben, and the four Benton children. "You didn't find Ruby?" she asked anxiously as Spud hurried toward her.

"Found where she'd been. She came walking barefoot up to a couple of houses. But the women there each had a houseful of kids too young to leave."

Brother Ben came up then and nodded. "They were sorry. They wanted to be neighborly, but they couldn't come," he said. "So both suggested she try another widow who lives a way back off the road."

"Apparently that's where Ruby went," Spud added, "but we can't be sure. There's no road, so we couldn't drive in, and we don't have a lantern or flashlight so we could walk in and check."

Hildy's mouth went dry. "What do you suppose happened to her?"

Spud and the old ranger shrugged.

"You don't think Mr. Kessick—"

"No, of course not!" Spud said emphatically.

Ben Strong nodded. "Kessick wouldn't dare!"

The doctor came up the stairs behind them. "I've got to be getting back," he said. "I'll look in again in a day or two. Meantime, someone's got to stay with her. Make her"—he glanced at the children's solemn, dirty faces—"make her see that she's got something worth sticking around for."

Without saying where he was going, the old ranger said he'd

be back as soon as possible and left with the doctor. Hildy guessed he was going to pay the doctor for his call.

Spud helped Hildy wash the four kids and bed them down on their old sagging mattress on the dirt floor. Hildy told Spud what the doctor had said as she placed a fresh, cool cloth on the widow's forehead.

The room grew quiet, and Hildy and Spud sat on two lug boxes at the upturned crate-table.

"Oh, Spud," Hildy whispered, "I haven't felt this way since my mother died."

Spud reached across the crate table past the lamp and awkwardly patted Hildy's hand. "This isn't your mother," he reminded her. "Mrs. Benton is not really your responsibility."

Hildy withdrew her hand quickly. "How can you say that?" she whispered hoarsely. "She's got no one! The kids aren't old enough to care for her. If she dies, they'll end up in an orphan's asylum. You've heard what terrible places they are."

"I know. Once, shortly after I . . . uh . . . left home and was really down on my luck, the police picked me up and sent me to one of those places."

Hildy's eyes grew wide. "What was it like?"

"Awful! It was an old two-story house that smelled terrible and looked worse. They fed us just enough to keep us alive—mostly oatmeal mush. Every meal. Hot for breakfast. Sliced cold for lunch and supper."

Spud's voice grew hard. "All the grown-ups were stonefaced and as unfeeling as a piece of steel. Everything was done on a schedule. Once a day, they lined up a bunch of little blue enamel pots in a row on the floor, something like an automobile assembly line . . ."

He paused and shifted uncomfortably, lowering his eyes, then finished. "Then they made all the children go potty together, whether they wanted to or not. At night, we older boys weren't allowed to get out of bed, no matter how desperately we needed to go. So there were accidents and punishments."

"Oh, Spud." Hildy reached across the table and touched his freckled hand.

His green eyes glistened with moisture, and his mouth almost quivered.

"I'm so sorry," Hildy apologized. "I didn't mean to bring up—"

"It's okay. I ran away. But sometimes I wonder about those who had to stay."

"We can't let that happen to these children." Hildy determined. She glanced down at the peaceful, sleeping little ones. "We just can't!"

"I didn't mean to upset you," Spud said a little sheepishly. "And I didn't mean you shouldn't care about Mrs. Benton. But you can't get so emotionally involved with this situation."

In the lamp's soft yellow glow, Hildy smiled down at the peaceful children again. "They remind me of my own sisters and baby brother when our mother died." Then turning her attention to Spud again, she said quickly, "Oh, Spud, don't you see? I'm already emotionally involved here."

Hildy sighed. *What should be done about Mrs. Benton?* she wondered. What could she possibly say that would help the widow rediscover the will to live? Hildy tried to place herself in the widow's situation and think how she must feel.

The woman knew her children needed her. But apparently Mrs. Benton was so discouraged and weary that even her responsibility and love for them had been overshadowed by the awesome burden of trying to support them. There were no agencies to help the family. However, if both parents were dead, at least the children would be fed and housed in the orphan's asylum.

"Maybe," Hildy whispered, "she's decided that the kids would be better off if she were dead."

"That's nonsense!" Spud snapped.

"Shh! Keep your voice down!" Hildy cautioned in a loud whisper. "You and I know that, but maybe Mrs. Benton doesn't. Not anymore. The doctor said she has been hungry and discouraged so long she can't think straight."

Spud took a long, slow breath before answering. "Well, you can't stay here and take care of her. You've got to help find Ruby."

"I know. It's a terrible thing to say, but I'm torn between wanting to help care for Mrs. Benton and her children, and finding my cousin."

"And helping Ruby find her father before August tenth."

"Oh, Spud, I don't know what to do!"

Just then the door squeaked open and Hildy and Spud looked up.

In the weak kerosene lamp Hildy saw two bare feet and a pair of overall pant legs on the top step. The feet started down the stairs.

A familiar voice said firmly, "I know what to do!"

Hildy and Spud jumped up, making the lamp rock on the table.

"Ruby!" Hildy cried.

CHAPTER EIGHTEEN

LONG, LONELY DAYS

S hh!" Ruby replied, stepping off the stairs onto the dirt floor. "Ye'll wake them kids."

Hildy rushed over and threw her arms around her cousin. "Where've you been, Ruby?"

"Now, don't go a-gittin' all mushy," Ruby scolded. She pulled away from Hildy's embrace and glanced over at the woman lying in the corner. "How's Mrs. Benton?"

The three young people walked over and gazed down at the pale, still woman on the pallet of blankets. Hildy told her cousin what the doctor had said, and Ruby sighed deeply, then turned back to the table and sat down. Hildy and Spud joined her.

"Now," Hildy said with irritation, "where've you been?"

Ruby's face looked pale and tired in the lamplight. "Had me a scare, I reckon."

Spud quickly sat forward. "What happened?"

"I went to fetch some help fer Mrs. Benton here. Couldn't nobody come. So I set out to another widder woman I heerd 'bout. She lived a way back off the road."

When Ruby paused, Hildy prompted, "And. . . .?"

"Took me a short cut along one of them little cliff-like places.

A gully. Full of ground squirrel holes and rocks and things. Including snakes."

Hildy shuddered. "Rattlesnakes?"

"You all right?" Spud asked.

"Am now, but they's only one thing in this world that skeers me senseless, and that's snakes! 'Specially rattlers. It took me a powerful long time to git back. Never did git to the widder woman's place."

Ruby glanced at Mrs. Benton. "Since I couldn't get no help fer this pore woman, I'm a-gonna stay here a spell," she added. "I'll do what I kin fer her'n the kids. When she's some better, and kin spare me, I'll ask around 'bout my daddy. I jist got to find him on time, ye know!"

Hildy started to protest.

"No," Ruby said firmly, "I done made up my mind, so when Brother Ben gits back, y'all go on home."

When the old ranger returned, he and the others briefly discussed their options. It was too late to try to find the bunkhouse Hildy's father had told them about, so they decided to drive back home. Telling Ruby goodbye, Hildy, Spud, and Brother Ben promised to come back and bring more food for the family as soon as they could. Then they left Ruby at the sod house with Mrs. Benton and the sleeping children.

It was after midnight when the Packard stopped in front of the Corrigans' barn-house. Hildy leaned forward in the backseat and put her hand on the old ranger's shoulder. "Good night, Brother Ben . . . Spud. Thanks for everything."

As she turned toward the barn-house a match flared inside. Hildy saw it reflected in the small window of the sliding glass door. The light settled into the steady, yellow glow of a coal oil lamp.

Just as the Packard turned around and headed back down the lane, Hildy's father eased the barn-house door open. He stood there in his nightshirt, holding the lamp.

"Thought it might be you," he said softly, sliding the door wide enough for her to enter. "You find Ruby?"

Hildy lowered her voice so she wouldn't waken her sisters

or baby brother. "Yes. She's fine. Going to stay with the widow Benton for a while. Did you find Mischief?"

"Sorry, honey. I talked to the Jarmans, but they said they didn't know anything about your coon. I don't know if they were telling the truth or not."

Hildy's hopes sank.

Molly sat up on the double bed mattress on the other side of the room and squinted at Hildy. "What happened to Ruby?" she asked with a yawn.

"It's a long story," Hildy said, stifling a yawn of her own. "I'll tell you in the morning."

When her father had blown out the lamp and returned to his bed, Hildy undressed in the dark. She quickly untied her long brown braids and let the tresses fall, knowing full well they'd be a rat's nest of tangles in the morning. But she was too tired to care. After saying her prayers, she eased into bed with her sisters.

She and Elizabeth slept with their heads at the top of the double mattress. Martha, Sarah and Iola, being smaller, slept at the foot of the bed, their bodies between their older sisters'. Hildy sometimes complained about the arrangement because the younger girls' toenails scratched the two older sister's legs every time the little ones rolled over. But she knew there was no other way until they had their "forever" home. Then they could have as many beds as they wanted.

Weary in mind and spirit, Hildy expected to drop off to sleep immediately, but she couldn't. Faces and fragments of the day's conversations flickered through her thoughts.

Her dad: "Ruby's disappeared—and so has your coon. . . . The Jarmans said they didn't know anything about Mischief."

Brother Ben: "Purpose. Plan. Persevere."

Jacob Benton: "Somethin' turrible's happened!"

Mrs. Benton: "I'm . . . so . . . tired."

The doctor: "She needs someone to give her a reason for living. Otherwise . . ."

Ruby: "I'll do what I kin fer Mrs. Benton an' the kids . . . I jist got to find my daddy on time!"

The final two words clanged through Hildy's mind like dull echoes. "On time! On time!"

When Hildy finally opened her eyes, she realized it was day-light. For a moment, she lay staring at the barn-house ceiling where a thread-waisted dauber was busy making mud cells. As she watched the wasp-like insect, Joey began his "hungry" cry, and Molly settled a saucepan on the wood-burning stove. Hildy missed hearing the clump of her father's boots and realized he had already been picked up for work.

Suddenly, Hildy remembered all the terrible happenings of the past few days. She leaped out of bed, and her sisters rolled over and mumbled in their sleep.

Molly turned from the stove where she was warming a bottle of milk in a saucepan of water. "'Morning, Hildy," she said cheerfully. "I don't remember you ever sleeping this late. You all right?"

Hildy took a few quick steps to the wall calendar. Her long hair flowed out behind her in a tangle of knots and flying ends. She skimmed the dates. "Today's Monday, July twenty-third. That leaves . . . nineteen days for Ruby to find her father."

"Want to talk about it while I give Joey his bottle?" Molly asked. She lifted the bottle from the saucepan, then made sure it wasn't too hot by shaking a few drops from the nipple against the inside of her bare arm.

Hildy nodded, took a deep breath, and ran her hands ab-sently across the knotted strands of hair. "So many things!" she said softly. "But I guess the only one I have any control over is looking for Mischief."

Molly picked up Joey and sat on the couch to give him his bottle.

Grabbing her brush, Hildy sat down beside them. As she began brushing out the tangled mass of hair, she told Molly about everything that had happened since leaving for the foot-hills the afternoon before.

Molly listened carefully while she fed the baby.

As Hildy finished her account, she shook her head. "I just

hope Mrs. Benton gets well and Ruby finds her father on time," she said. "Molly, I've got to go back and help as soon as possible!"

"I understand," Molly replied with a knowing smile. "Meanwhile, I've learned something that may help you find Mischief."

Hildy quit brushing her hair and turned to face her stepmother.

"Late yesterday," Molly continued, "a couple of boys came over to play with your sisters. They live near the river, I guess, and they said they'd heard hounds baying there."

"You mean on the trail of a coon? Maybe Mischief?"

"The river's not too far, and raccoons love water, you know."

"There must be lots of raccoons along the river bottom."

"But they're night creatures. These boys said the hounds were running in daylight."

Hildy's heart beat faster. "Mischief runs around in the daytime, same as night," she said with a grin. "I'll check it out."

Later that morning, Hildy and Elizabeth walked down to the river. They looked all around for tracks, especially on sand bars, where they could be easily seen. When the girls found a couple of boys fishing, they asked them if they had seen or heard any sign of a raccoon or hounds running. They hadn't.

Discouraged, Hildy and Elizabeth returned home, and Elizabeth headed straight to the girls' bed. When she pulled back the pillow from the foot of the bed, Hildy saw a piece of red and green hard candy on the sheetless mattress.

Elizabeth sighed. "It's from last Christmas," she explained. "I saved it in a Mason jar with the lid on so Mischief couldn't smell it. I put that candy under the pillow this morning, hoping she'd come find it while we were gone."

Hildy hugged her sister. "She'll turn up. We've got to believe that." Remembering what Brother Ben had said, she added, "Our purpose is to find Mischief. Let's make a plan and then act on it until we get her back. We've got to persevere."

"Persevere?" Elizabeth repeated the word uncertainly. "I bet that's one of the words you learned from Spud's dictionary."

"Actually, I learned it from Brother Ben. He taught me three

words, really: purpose, plan, and persevere. Come on. Let's ask
Martha and Sarah if they'd like to help."

"And Iola?"

"She's pretty small, but why not? Let's share with all of them.
Someday, those three words are going to help us get our 'forever' home, too."

The plan to find Mischief was simple, but it took time to
carry it out. Each day the older girls printed homemade signs:
Lost: Pet Raccoon. Friendly. May Be Seen in Daytime. Named
Mischief.

The girls couldn't offer a reward, so they just included their
names and address.

They posted signs on poles, fence posts, and tree trunks
everywhere. Day after day they asked questions in a different
direction, walking sometimes a mile between ranch houses.
When there was no encouragement, the days became long and
lonely. The nights were worse.

When one of the neighbors offered Molly a lift into town on
Saturday, the five sisters took new signs and rode along. They
posted signs everywhere, including leaving some in the window
of every business, plus the police and fire stations.

While they were in town, they also stopped by the church
and told the minister about how sick Mrs. Benton was. Pastor
Hyde agreed to coordinate an effort to get more food out to the
widow and her children.

That night Joe Corrigan came home again in the boss's
pickup. Hildy's father had been working such long hours that
he hadn't had time to look for a car. However, now the situation
was changing. He told his family he would be working at the
ranch outside of town for a few days. Since he would be home
nights, he would have a better chance of finding a car in the
valley.

On Sunday morning, Brother Ben came up to Hildy after the
church service. "How's it going?" he asked, flipping his white
moustache.

Hildy smiled up at the tall old ranger. "We've done the first
two. Now we're persevering."

He frowned, then smiled. "I see. Well, you ought to be seeing some results soon, I hope."

"Me, too. Tuesday's the last day of the month. It's been a week now with no sign of Mischief. We're all heartsick."

"I understand. That's one special coon."

"I've been thinking about Ruby, though," Hildy said, absently shaking hands older people extended to her. "And Mrs. Benton and the kids. I wish there were some way to find out how she's doing."

"I can get away Thursday for a drive to Thunder Mountain," the old ranger told her. "Want to ride along?"

"Of course! Oh, how about Spud?"

"He's welcome, too."

Shortly after sunup on August second, Ben Strong came by the barn-house for Hildy. Spud was already in the Packard's front seat, and Lindy was jumping around in the back. Molly took the dog and Hildy slid into the backseat. She was happy to see a bag of groceries on the floor on the other side of the car.

Spud turned around. "Any word on Mischief?" he asked.

"Not a thing," Hildy said with a sigh.

As Brother Strong drove off, Hildy noticed the previous day's *Sacramento Bee* newspaper lying on the seat beside her. She picked it up and skimmed the front page, shaking her head. In Germany, President Von Hindenburg was dying. Chancellor Adolph Hitler had announced plans to be both president and chancellor. This would make him absolute dictator, the paper said.

She sighed again. "Nothing but bad news," she said. "Maybe I'd better look at ads for cars. Daddy sure needs one."

"Be my guest," the old ranger said.

As Hildy scanned the ad section, she noticed several cars listed for thirty-five to fifty-five dollars. She read aloud, "A 1927 four-door Essex, a '26 Dodge, and a '26 Studebaker. And here's a '28 Willys Knight coupe for a little more."

The old ranger glanced back at her. "Take the paper home to your father tonight," he suggested.

Spud turned around and smiled at her. "Why don't you

check the real estate ads?" he said. "Maybe you'll find your 'forever' home listed in there."

Hildy turned to the proper page. "Not many for sale," she said. "Here's a three-bedroom house for $4,150 and a six-room house for $5,950." She threw the paper down on the seat. "We could never afford that much money!"

Brother Strong looked at her in the rearview mirror. "You forgetting what we talked about the other day?"

Hildy flushed. "Got to watch what I say, huh?"

"And what you think," the old ranger reminded her. "Especially that."

Hildy lapsed into silence, and Spud and Brother Ben didn't say any more either. A relaxed, pleasant silence lasted until the Packard turned off the highway by Shaw's Ferry.

Hildy looked up at Thunder Mountain, its bulky mass thrusting into the sky. Somehow Hildy felt threatened by it.

She leaned forward and rested her hand on the top of the front seat. "Brother Ben," she said, "what're you going to do after we check on Ruby and Mrs. Benton?"

"There are several things we could do," the old ranger replied. "First, of course, I hope Ruby's found her father. But if she hasn't, I'd like to help her look."

Spud nodded. "We could start by trying to find the sheepherder the lion hunter told about," he suggested. "He might be able to tell us where Nate Konning is."

Hildy shook her head. "Even if Ruby and Mrs. Benton are all right, there'd be no time to do that today."

The old ranger reached his left hand across his right shoulder and patted her hand. "We've got eight days left, counting next Saturday and Sunday," he calmly reminded her. "Six working days if we include Friday the tenth."

Hildy frowned. "Even if Mrs. Benton's better and Ruby's not too discouraged about finding her father, there's still one more problem."

Spud raised one eyebrow. "You mean, where's Nate Konning going to get the money to pay off the mortgage?"

Hildy looked at the old ranger's eyes in the rearview mirror.

"Maybe I shouldn't ask, but has Ruby said anything about borrowing the money from you, Brother Ben?"

"No, but I suspect she might."

Hildy didn't feel she could ask him if he would make the payment to save the ranch.

As the Packard turned off the dirt road into the dusty lane leading to Thunder Mountain, Hildy turned to look toward the sod house. Through the dusty windshield, she saw another car parked there already.

Her heart beat faster. "Who do you suppose that is?" she asked with sudden anxiety. "The doctor?"

"I don't know," Brother Ben replied, "but the Benton kids have heard us. And from the way they're running, I think something's wrong again!"

CHAPTER NINETEEN

A STRANGE TWIST

Jacob outran his three younger sisters and leaped up on the Packard's running board the moment the car stopped. Thrusting his frightened face in the driver's side window, he spoke rapidly. "Come quick!" he cried out of breath. "They're a-tryin' to throw us off'n the place!"

Hildy threw open the back door and leaped out. "Who is?" she demanded.

The little Benton girls crowded around Hildy, and grabbed anxiously at both hands, holding on tightly.

Seth jumped off the running board. "Some man," he said. "An' his boy. Hurry!" He turned and sprinted back toward the house.

Holding the younger two girls' hands, Hildy hurried after him. Soon she heard Ruby's angry voice from inside the sod house door. The words were muffled, but her strident tone pierced the air.

Suddenly, the cellar-like door burst open. Ozzell Kessick and his nephew scrambled out.

Ruby followed close behind, wielding a relic of a broom. She kept smacking both uncle and nephew, in turn, on their behinds.

"Ow!" Rob hollered as the broom caught him again and again. "Uncle Oz, she's killing me!"

Neither Ruby nor the Kessicks seemed to notice the visitors until they were a few feet away.

Brother Ben called out to the troublemakers. "Hold on there, you two! Stand right there!" The authority in his tone halted the fleeing Kessicks. Ruby froze with her broom in midair.

As Spud and Hildy came up beside the old ranger, he took charge of the situation. "What's this all about?" he demanded.

Clutching the broom in both hands, Ruby told her friends what was happening. "Oh, Brother Ben! They're a-sayin' we got to git outta here 'cause they're the new owners!" she cried. "Only I tol' them they ain't yet. Mrs. Benton's too poorly to run these polecats off, so I'm a-doin' it myself! Now make 'em scat afore I ruin their backsides complete!"

Hildy almost smiled in spite of the gravity of the situation. "You okay, Ruby?" she asked. "And Mrs. Benton?"

Ruby motioned toward the open door. "Come inside and see fer yoreself," she answered. "Brother Strong, air ye a-gonna make these two varmits skedaddle?"

"I want to talk to them first," the old ranger replied. "Hildy, why don't you go check on Mrs. Benton? Spud and I will be down in a minute."

Ruby led Hildy down the stairs, and Hildy was surprised at the change in the dugout's interior. Small windows Hildy hadn't seen before stood open. Fresh air and sunlight streamed in. Everything had been dusted and straightened. There was a faint smell of earth, so Hildy guessed Ruby had been sweeping the dirt floor when the Kessicks arrived.

Then Hildy saw the widow sitting on an upturned lug box, her hair combed and put up in a bun. "Mrs. Benton!" she exclaimed in surprise. Though still barefooted, the woman's faded dress had been freshly laundered. And her face! The sad, discouraged look was gone. Her eyes almost sparkled behind her rimless eye glasses. "What happened? You look . . . different!"

The woman smiled. "Reckon the good Lord seen I had stood 'bout all I could stand, so He sent me an angel to cheer me up."

She reached over and took Ruby's hand.

Rachel smiled up at Hildy. "Us, too," she said, spinning around rapidly. "Ruby washed an' patched our dresses." Grabbing the hem of her whirling skirt, she started to lift it. "See? We even got clean—"

"That's enough, Rachel," Ruby said quickly. She reached over and put the little girl's skirt down. "Now, all of you go outside and play. But don't bother Brother Strong and the others, please!"

Jacob looked up at Hildy. "Some church folk brung us more food, and Ruby made Ma eat good," he said with satisfaction. "She patched knees on my pants, too. See?" He touched his clean overalls. "An' I hauled all the water fer ever'thing," he said proudly. "Likely to of drained the crick, Ruby used so much."

Hildy patted the boy's shoulder. "You did great."

As the children ran up the stairs Hildy heard the Kessicks' car drive away. Then Spud came down the steps followed by Brother Strong.

The old ranger removed his white hat and held it in his hands. "Howdy, Mrs. Benton. You're looking mighty perky." She smiled and he turned to Ruby. "Kessick and his nephew won't be back for a while, but they're not through."

"I shoulda whupped 'em good!" Ruby said.

Hildy smiled. "I think you did quite enough!"

Spud hitched up his breeches. "Brother Strong told Kessick that he was going to loan you the money, Ruby, so you could pay off the ranch."

Ruby's mouth dropped open. She looked at the old ranger in disbelief. "Ye done that?"

Spud answered for him. "He did, but Kessick said that won't work because he's talked to Nate Konning, and—"

"He's talked to my daddy?" Ruby cried. "Whar is he?"

Brother Strong lowered his head slightly. "He wouldn't say, but now we know for sure he's all right and that he's nearby."

Hildy turned to Spud anxiously. "What'd you mean, Spud?

Why did Mr. Kessick say Brother Strong can't loan Ruby the money?"

The old ranger twirled the brim of his white hat through his big fingers. "According to Kessick, Ruby's father says he has no daughter. Under the terms of the contract, only Nate Konning or his heir can pay—"

" 'Course he don't know I'm his daughter!" Ruby interrupted. "He don't know 'bout me yet!"

"He does now," Spud told her. "Kessick told him. But if Konning denies you're related, you can't pay off the mortgage even if Brother Strong loans you the money."

"Then I jist gotta find my daddy fast an' tell him all 'bout me," Ruby resolved.

The old ranger looked thoughtful. "Ruby, when you do find Nate Konning, how're you going to convince him you really are his daughter?"

"Why, I'll jist tell him!"

Spud cocked his head. "Suppose he won't believe you?"

Ruby spun on him, her voice sharp. " 'Course he'll believe me!"

"But can you prove it?" Spud persisted.

"Whar's my broom?" Ruby yelped. "I'll whup you good with it, Spud. Same's I did them Kessicks."

Hildy reached out and grabbed Ruby's hand. "Easy, now. Spud's not trying to make you angry. He's only asking a reasonable question."

Brother Strong nodded. "Why don't we all sit down and think this through?" he suggested. "Then let's see if we can find Nate Konning in the time we've got left. Otherwise, next Saturday morning, you can be sure Kessick will be out here with the sheriff to evict everyone from this place."

When the others agreed and found a place to sit, the old ranger turned to Ruby. "Mind if I ask some questions?"

" 'Course not, Brother Strong," she replied. "But shouldn't we oughta be out a-lookin' fer my daddy? Drive over to that sheepherder's camp the lion hunter told us 'bout?"

After a short discussion, they all agreed that might be the

best next step. Bidding goodbye to the Bentons and leaving the groceries they had brought, Ruby and the others got back into the old ranger's Packard.

As they drove south along the looming black cliffs of Thunder Mountain, Ben Strong looked at Ruby in the rearview mirror. "These questions may be hard for you to answer, but I've got to know a few things about you, Ruby," he said. "For instance, do you have a birth certificate?"

"Never thought 'bout one."

"What was your mother's maiden name?"

"Beulah Skaggs. She died when I was a baby."

"So all you know about either of your parents is what people told you?"

"I reckon. My Grandma Skaggs told me that my ma said my daddy was pizened with mustard gas when he was a so-jer in France durin' the war. She said he died jist afore I was borned. But I didn't believe that."

"Your Grandmother Skaggs would have been your father's mother-in-law, then. So did she ever meet him?"

"Nope. She told me that my ma done left home when she was 'bout sixteen. Went to Texas. Didn't write ner nothin'. When she come back couple years later, she said she met her husbun' at a camp meetin'. But they separated and my ma come back to the Ozarks. A few months later, I was borned."

"So your grandmother raised you." The old ranger tapped his fingers on the steering wheel thoughtfully. "Did she ever say whether she believed Beulah's story or not?"

"Sometimes Gram was about as mean as her sister," Ruby said with a sigh. "That's Hildy's Granny Dunnigan. Them sisters hated each other. Gram's o'nry, but Hildy's Granny Dunnigan is worser. She's the one 'as said the most meanest, most contrary things 'bout me."

Ruby raised her voice. "She called me a woods colt and told folks I didn't have no daddy, legal-like," she said in pain and anger. "Ever'body in them thar hills looked down their noses at me. But when I find my daddy, we're a-gonna go back thar an' I'll rub their noses in the dirt!"

Hildy ached for Ruby. Silently, she reached over and took her cousin's hand.

Brother Ben glanced back at the girls and continued. "When did you set your heart on finding the truth about your father, Ruby?"

The girl shrugged and looked at her cousin. "When do ye reckon that was?"

Hildy thought a moment. "Well, it had to have been after we left the Ozarks looking for Molly and the kids. I remember shortly after you and I met Spud, you said you were wishing you knew for sure if your pa was alive or dead."

"I 'member that," Ruby said.

"Then I think it was when we were riding in our first automobile that you said, 'I wish I had a daddy.' Then you said all you really wanted to know was the truth. But a few seconds later, you told me that wasn't exactly right, either. You said, 'I'd sure like to find him—if he's alive.' Remember, Ruby?"

Her cousin nodded.

Spud turned around in surprise. "You sure do have a good memory, Hildy, to remember all that," he said in obvious admiration.

Hildy felt her face turning red, and she was glad when Brother Ben continued with his questions.

"Where'd you get the snapshot you carry of Nate Konning?" the old ranger asked.

"In Oklahoma," Ruby replied. "Hildy and me was a-stayin' with some folks named Witt. They remembered a rider worked for them with the same last name as mine. So when Hildy and me was a-leavin', Mrs. Witt give me this pi'tcher. It's marked on the back, 'Highpockets Konning, 1921.' "

Brother Ben probed gently. "But you don't know if that snapshot is really of your father?"

"Well, them Kessicks shore got riled when they seen that pi'tcher!" Ruby defended herself. "An' the way they're a-actin' an' sayin' they'd seed him shore proves to me that that's a pi'tcher of my very own daddy. When we find him, he'll reco'nize hisself, an' that'll be that!"

The old man's voice was tender as he continued. "I hope so, Ruby. But I need to ask some more questions of both you and your cousin." He flipped his mustache thoughtfully. "Hildy, did your father, Ruby's Uncle Joe, ever mention meeting Nate Konning?"

"No, not that I remember."

"But he knew Ruby's mother, Beulah?"

"Yes, of course," Hildy replied. "Relatives in the Ozarks all knew each other."

"But nobody could give testimony to support Ruby's claim about Nate Konning being her father. Certainly the Kessicks would demand proof. And they probably wouldn't accept anything unless it was proven in court."

Spud turned and frowned at the old ranger. "But Kessick would already have the ranch," he said. "It'd be too late."

Ruby slumped in the seat. "Shore would. Too late fer ever'-body!"

Hildy felt sick for Ruby. Even though it was a bright, sun-shiny day, the atmosphere was bleak inside the Packard. Hildy turned sad eyes to look out the window.

On the right, gently rolling hills looked barren and bleak. On the left, Thunder Mountain rose like a miles-long medieval castle. Somewhere out there, closer to where the dynamite explosions prepared for the build of an irrigation dam, Nate Konning was working. But where?

As the Packard rolled along down the road, Ruby sighed. "I shoulda knowed things was a-goin' too good," she said softly. "Mrs. Benton an' her kids was treatin' me like a queen. Right away, it was kinda like we was family, ye know? So soon's I found my daddy, we was all gonna have us a big celebration. Only now it's like wakin' up an' findin' ye was a-dreamin'."

"Not necessarily," Spud argued, turning around again. "There's that picture Mrs. Benton showed you—the one she found in the sod house . . ."

Ruby jumped up so suddenly she almost hit her head on the low canvas roof. "I plumb forgot that!" she cried. "It's the same as the one my grandma has of my ma."

Spud pounded his fist excitedly on the backseat. "Then Nate Konning is your father!" Instantly his smile faded. "But if you don't find him, the Kessicks will never let that snapshot stop them from taking possession of the ranch on August tenth!"

Brother Strong glanced back at the girls again. "And, Ruby, you don't have your mother's picture from the Ozarks," he reminded her, "and the Kessicks aren't going to take your word for it. Besides, it'd take a trial to introduce your mother's photograph as evidence. Then it'd be far too late!"

Ruby slumped down in her seat again. "Reckon yore right."

Hildy looked at her cousin with concern. "But none of that's necessary if we find your father," she said, feeling hope revive again.

"Yore right!" Ruby sat upright again. "That's all we got to do."

"No," Spud said quietly, "we've not only got to find him, we have to get him to the courthouse to pay off the mortgage before five o'clock on August tenth. That's only eight days from now. And we're assuming that you'd still loan the money, Brother Ben?"

"My offer stands," he assured them.

Ruby looked determined again. "Then what're we a-waitin' fer?" she asked. "Brother Ben, stomp yore foot plumb through them floorboards. We got to find that other sheepherder right away!"

This time they were not turned back by a flagman or a closed road. In the distance they heard one heavy explosion from where the dam was being built. But they had no trouble finding the high ridge the lion hunter had described.

As soon as Brother Strong stopped the car, the foursome quickly got out. Eagerly, they crawled through the barbed wire fence and followed a shallow wash westward, away from the mountain.

They hadn't gone more than a half mile when they found the sheep camp. Hildy's hopes soared when she saw the herder beyond his canvas-covered wagon. The man stood up as his dogs announced the coming of visitors.

Hildy grabbed Ruby's hand excitedly. "Oh, I hope he speaks English," she said.

Moments later, with the small sheep dogs trailing, the visitors stopped in front of the herder. He was a short, strongly built man with a lean, unshaven face. Without speaking, he examined the visitors through narrowed eyes that had been squinting at a blazing landscape for too long.

Ruby already had her snapshot in hand when Ben Strong introduced himself and the others. Then he told the man why they had come.

The herder looked at the picture. "Looks like the guy who owns the sod house. I helped build his barn."

"Whar is he?" Ruby blurted.

"Got a camp east and south." The herder pointed toward Thunder Mountain.

Hildy could hardly keep from yelling with joy.

The sheepherder shrugged. "Nobody in his right mind would work so close to where they're blowin' up that mountain, but he don't seem to care much."

"How'll we find him?" Brother Strong asked.

The man picked up a stick and squatted in front of them. "I'll draw a map," he said. Quickly, he sketched in the dirt, explaining as he went. Then he straightened and dropped the stick. "Watch out for rattlers and mind you don't go in when them red flags is flyin'. Means they're gonna blow up more of that mountain."

They all thanked the sheepherder and happily headed back toward the car.

Ruby's face was radiant. "I'm a-gonna find my daddy! He's jist yonder!" she exclaimed. "Brother Ben, kin we go thar now?"

"First, we'll have to see if the red flags are flying," the old ranger said.

Hildy should have been happy, too, but she wasn't. From the moment she had first seen Thunder Mountain, she had been uneasy. Now it loomed like a black, threatening monster waiting for her and the others to come closer. Hildy was suddenly afraid—very afraid—but she wasn't sure why.

CHAPTER TWENTY

A TERRIBLE DISCOVERY

Back in the car, Hildy leaned forward and anxiously peered out the dusty windshield. As they drove on, she saw something on the left fenceposts in the distance.

She gasped and pointed. "Red flags!" she cried. "And signs: Danger! Explosives! No Trespassing!" She glanced up at Thunder Mountain. It still waited in threatening silence.

Ruby raised her eyebrows. "It's safe enough fer them men yonder," she insisted. "Let's go talk to 'em."

Brother Ben pulled up alongside two workmen in silvery hard hats. They wore heavy leather gloves to string extra barbed wire on the fence on the Thunder Mountain side.

The nearest man came over when the Packard stopped. "See them signs and red flags?" he began in an irritated tone. "That means they're going to dynamite the whole face off this thing." He waved a gloved hand toward Thunder Mountain. "You folks better vamoose, fast!"

Ruby leaned out the back window and pointed at Thunder Mountain. "My father's in thar! We've got to git to him."

"Nobody's been back in there for days except powder monkeys, drilling and placing the dynamite. Well, there was a sheepherder, but he was warned to get out."

"Have ye seed 'im come out?" Ruby asked anxiously.

"I'm not his keeper," the man said with a shrug. "Unless he's crazy, he came out. But I didn't see him."

"Kin we go in and look?" Ruby asked anxiously.

"Sorry, young lady, not today." The workman straightened up and turned around.

"Then when?" she called desperately.

"About two weeks."

"But that's too late!" Ruby wailed.

"Look," the man growled. He turned around again and raised his voice. "I'm busy. You either get going, or I call the sheriff on all of you."

Hildy felt mixed relief and concern as the Packard turned around and headed for the sod house. In the backseat, she leaned over to her cousin. "Promise me you won't try to go in there while we're gone."

Ruby pursed her lips. "I'll check ever' day to see if they take them red flags down. If'n they don't, come August tenth—I'm a-goin' in anyways!"

Nothing any of the others said could change Ruby's mind. They left her with the Bentons and headed back for the valley.

On the drive home, Brother Ben was still trying to sort out all the facts about Ruby and her family. "Hildy," he began, "since your father knew Ruby's mother, did he ever tell you about how Beulah and Nate Konning met?"

Hildy leaned forward in the backseat. "Well, Daddy told me he met Beulah through her cousin, Elizabeth, before she and Daddy got married."

"Elizabeth was your late mother?"

"Yes." Hildy nodded. "Well, Beulah and her mother—Ruby's grandmother—had a big quarrel one day. Beulah went to Texas. Months later, she came back to the Ozarks alone. Beulah told everybody, including Daddy, that she'd met Nate at a camp meeting, married, then separated. Ruby was born about six months later, so apparently her father never knew about her. My daddy never met Nate Konning."

It was dusk when the Packard turned into the Corrigan drive-way. Hildy's father, stepmother, and siblings came out to meet them.

Hildy's sisters immediately told her the sad news that they had not found the pet raccoon yet. Her father hadn't been able to find a car, either.

Hildy tried to hide her disappointment about both, especially Mischief.

Spud patted the back of her hand and smiled. "We'll keep looking until we find that coon," he assured her.

Brother Ben put on his white hat. "Well, we've got to go, but we'll plan on going back up to help Ruby look soon's I can get away."

Hildy swallowed hard. "Even if we can get up there before, I just can't stand not knowing what'll happen on August tenth," she confessed.

"That's a week from tomorrow. I'll get you there that day, somehow, Hildy. Meanwhile, I hope you find your coon."

"I'm going to see if I can find out anything from Jarmans about her," Hildy said.

The next morning after her father had been picked up for work, Hildy walked over to the Jarman's place. It was a one-room tarpaper shack with a lean-to in the back. Beyond that, the tank house and outhouse leaned precariously. Hens cackled from the sagging chicken house. Old tires, parts from cars, wagons, buggies, and farm machinery were partially hidden by brown, knee-high weeds.

A black and tan hound bayed thunderously as the girl walked barefoot toward the tangled remains of what had once been a picket fence. Hildy glanced around anxiously for the second dog. She had always seen it whenever the Jarmans' pickup had been around.

"Hey!" The fierce shout from inside made the dog stop barking and plunge under the high front porch. A moment later, Charley Jarman pushed open the rusted screen door. It slammed shut behind him. Fishing his chewing tobacco from his overall bib pocket, he watched in disapproving silence as the girl cautiously approached.

She stopped at the bottom step and looked up. "Mr. Jarman, sir, I'm Hildy Corrigan and I live—"

"I know! What d'yuh want?" His tone was harsh.

"I know you've been asked before, but—"

"No, I ain't seen yore pet coon! What's more, if I did, I'd sic muh dawg on it and send ye the tail!"

Hildy felt a sudden wave of nausea that seemed to stop in her throat. She swallowed hard, her eyes still riveted on her uncouth neighbor. "I'm sorry about your eggs being stolen and your dog being cut up, but Mischief—"

Again, the man interrupted with a growl. "I know yore coon didn't do them things, girlie."

A shadow appeared inside the screen door and Rafe Jarman called out to her. "Wisht it hadda, though. Now Ol' Blue's daid on accounta it *wasn't* yore coon."

Hildy shook her head, her long brown braids flying. "I—I don't understand."

" 'Course ye don't!" the boy yelled. "Pa ketched Ol' Blue a-doin' it. He was a wu'thless, no-'count, aig-suckin' dog. Well, he ain't no more!"

Afraid to ask why not, Hildy ran her tongue along her lips. They suddenly felt very dry. "I'm . . . sorry."

"Don't be." The thin coon hunter's tone softened. He shifted the wad of chewing tobacco to his other cheek. "Fool dawg got infected from that big tomcat's claws, anyway."

"Big tomcat?"

Rafe pushed the door open. "Y'all musta seen him hereabouts. Big booger, and meaner'n sin."

Hildy nodded. She remembered when the yellow tom's claws slashed Mischief's nose. The coon had spent hours on the barn's highest peak.

"Ketched 'em both the same day," Mr. Jarman said, spraying an ugly stream of tobacco at a passing orange-and-black butterfly. "Y'all got no cause to think 'bout them two no more."

Hildy shivered slightly. "Well," she said, turning to go, "Sorry about your dog. Sorry to have bothered you, too."

"Hey, girlie!"

She turned back to look at the man, fearful of what he might say or do.

"Don't y'all go gittin' no idees I'm soft on muh word. I done tol' ye that I'd see yore coon daid. If'n I ever do see him, I'll do it. But I give yuh muh bonded word—neither me ner Rafe's seen that coon."

Hildy believed him. As she left, she felt sick inside. *Will I ever see Mischief again?* she wondered.

The next several days dragged for Hildy. She constantly searched for the coon, all the while wondering how Ruby was doing.

On August ninth, when Hildy could hardly stand the suspense, she heard Spud's whistle and ran outside.

"Hi, Hildy!" Spud said as he crawled through the barbed wire. "The neighbor with the phone just drove over to my tree house with a message. Brother Ben says he'll be here about four o'clock in the morning! We're going to see Ruby! Can you be ready?"

When the big alarm clock went off at three-thirty, Hildy leaped up, her heart racing, eager to be on her way. She was dressed and ready when the Packard's lights turned into the lane promptly at four o'clock.

Shortly after dawn, the car stopped in front of the sod house. Hildy sighed with relief as Ruby threw open the cellar-like door. "I kinda figgered y'all'd be up early," she said, sticking her head through the Packard's open window. "Well, it's now er never. Scoot over, Hildy, and let's git a-goin'!"

On the drive south along the looming black mass of Thunder Mountain, Ruby explained what had happened since they'd last been together. "I checked ever' day, and them red flags was up," she said. "But even if they're still thar this mornin,' I'm a-goin' in, one way er another. Gonna find me my daddy. Ain't nobody or nothin' goin' to stop me, neither."

"Look!" Spud exclaimed. "On the fence posts to the left. No flags! Looks as if we're in luck."

Brother Strong parked the Packard a couple hundred yards ahead of where they had been turned back the week before.

They all crawled through the barbed wire and started up a small dry wash toward Thunder Mountain.

Earlier, the old ranger had proven his physical condition for his age, so Hildy didn't concern herself with his stamina while they approached the dark, dense basalt rock mass.

Now, as the top of Thunder Mountain turned a bright glow from the sun rising on the other side, her heart pounded as though trying to break her ribs. She wasn't sure if it was excitement, exertion, or fear.

She stopped to rest. "I thought that last week the man said they were going to blow the whole face of this mountain off."

"Well, they didn't, so hesh up an' keep movin'!" Ruby answered a little sharply.

Hildy wasn't offended. She understood her cousin's testiness. When she turned to look back toward the Packard, she gasped. "Whew! We've already come a long way," she said. "See how little that truck looks down on the roadway?"

Below them, the same pickup they had seen the week before was parked on the road. The two workmen with silvery hats got out of the truck, talking animatedly and waving their arms wildly. A few minutes later they jumped back into the truck and sped off.

Hildy didn't think much about it. "Guess they forgot their tools or something," she told herself. Turning her attention back to the climb, she followed Ben Strong, Ruby, and Spud toward Thunder Mountain.

Soon they came to a small ravine near the base of the great volcanic mountain. The cliffs apparently had been formed by an ancient river. The sides rose about fifty feet into the air, with infrequent recesses, like small, shallow caves.

Even though the sun would not touch this side of the mountain for hours, the ground squirrels scurried about, sounding their alarm whistles. Hildy knew the rattlers would also be stirring, so she remained doubly alert.

A few minutes later, she scrambled onto a large boulder and looked around. "I still don't see any sign of his camp, and the ravine runs both ways. Which should we take?"

"Ain't no time to be wrong," Ruby said.

Spud nodded. "At least, we should be about through climbing. Should be easier now, no matter which way we go."

"I know. We split up," Ruby suggested. "Two of us go each way. The one that don't find his camp comes back hyar and follows the way the others already went."

"Better still," Spud said, "whoever finds him or his camp sends one person back here to lead the others."

"That sounds like a good idea," Brother Strong replied.

They all agreed. Ruby and the old ranger turned north, following the ancient riverbed. Hildy and Spud headed south, walking along the rocky, dry wash for about a hundred yards, where it curved around a bend. There Hildy and Spud stopped.

"Now what?" Hildy asked. "There's a Y ahead. Both paths seem to lead down into an open meadow. Which should we try?"

"You take the one on the right. I'll take the other. Whoever finds anything, give a shout. We'll be close enough to hear."

Hildy was a little hesitant to be separated in such desolate country. But she didn't want Spud to know that, so she turned to the right.

Almost at once, the terrible, vast loneliness nearly overwhelmed her. She was still in the deep shadows of Thunder Mountain, but a short distance ahead to the west, the empty brown, barren hills ran endlessly toward the horizon.

The sharp, unpleasant odor of tarweed stung her nostrils, and perspiration trickled down her face. A fine sand gritted in her teeth and dried her tongue.

"Lonely life," she told herself, hurrying along as fast as she dared, still alert for danger. "I could never be a sheepherder."

She rounded another curve and stopped short. "There!" The word seemed snatched away as though unseen forces resented a word in the vast silent void.

She first saw the weathered, canvas-topped wagon. There was a gaping hole in the top where a stovepipe had been removed. However, there were no sheep or dogs. The herder sat alone on the wagon tongue, his back to her.

"Uh, mister . . ." Hildy called out, hoping she wouldn't startle the man. "Mr. Nate Konning?"

The sheepherder spun around and leaped to his feet in one movement, dropping a piece of stovepipe with a hollow clatter. Tall and slender, the man wore faded hickory-striped overalls, scuffed cowboy boots with walking heels, and a sweaty tapered cowboy hat.

"What the—" He stopped abruptly. "Well, I'll be dogged. A girl!" As he swept his hat off in an automatic gesture of respect, his long, untidy blond hair spilled over both sides of his unshaven face.

Suddenly, he stiffened and his voice rose. "What're ye a-doin' up here? Don't ye know they're a-gonna blow the face off'n this mountain?"

"They took the signs down." Hildy frowned, coming closer. "I've seen you somewhere—oh!" Shocking realization cut off her words.

"An' I reckon I know ye, too," he said with a grin. When he smiled, he reminded Hildy of someone. She couldn't quite think who. "Yore the little lady that come to my rescue in Simple Justice when them kids was a-pesterin' me 'bout my hat!"

Hildy was both surprised and embarrassed. She changed the subject quickly. "Are you Nate Konning?"

The man's smile faded and he spoke defensively. "Who wants to know?"

"I'm your niece, Hildy Corrigan. Your daughter's looking for you. She's right over there." Hildy pointed back toward the curve.

"Ozzie Kessick a'ready tol' me about some gal a-claimin' to be my kin, but I ain't got no daughter!"

"Oh, but you have," Hildy told him. "Her name's Ruby. She's Beulah's daughter. Yours and Beulah's—she was Beulah Skaggs before you married."

The tall man staggered with this information. His mouth worked a moment before words came. Then he said hoarsely, "If I had me a daughter—which I ain't—I never want to see her! Now, go away and leave me alone!"

CHAPTER TWENTY-ONE

TERROR ON THUNDER MOUNTAIN

Hildy reeled. "You can't mean that?"

"I shore do! I ain't got no daughter, so go away afore this mountain blows up." Nate Konning picked up the stovepipe he'd dropped and turned his back on Hildy.

She stood there, stunned. "You can't reject your own daughter!" she protested.

He picked up a pair of pliers and began crimping one end of the new stovepipe. "This mountain's goin' to blow, I tol' ye! Now git!"

Hildy had been afraid of Thunder Mountain almost from the first time she saw it. Now, at its base she had a greater fear. The strong-willed nature that was both her strength and her weakness shot passion through Hildy. She flushed with anger and took a couple of quick steps to face the man.

"Look at me!" she snapped, her voice sharp. When he kept on working with the stovepipe, Hildy reached out and slapped it from his hand. "I said, look at me!"

He started to reach for the clattering stovepipe, but Hildy

kicked it away. "Don't you have any feelings? No desire to see her?"

"I tol' ye—"

"Is your name Nate Konning?" Hildy demanded. When he nodded, she raged on. "And did you marry Beulah Skaggs about fourteen years ago?"

"Yes," he admitted. "We met at a Texas camp meeting, but—"

"You separated. She went home to the Ozarks, and you never saw her again. Right?"

"I heard she . . . died."

"She did. But not before she gave birth to a little girl. That's Ruby—your own daughter. She's suffered for years because of the terrible things people said—that her father wasn't dead, that she had no father because she was a woods colt. After all those awful hurts, Ruby wanted to know the truth. Were you alive or dead? Had her mother really been married?"

Hildy took a deep breath and continued. "Ruby's been rejected all her life because of you. She's set out to find you, risking her life! Now the search is over, but you're rejecting her, too! Her own father? I can't tell her that. It'll kill her!"

Slowly, the man's face puckered under the unshaven beard. His mouth began to quiver and tears sprang to his eyes. "I didn't know . . ."

"I understand that," Hildy conceded, softening a little at the sign of caring. "But now you do know. She's right over there beyond that curve, next to—"

"My Lord!" Nate Konning leaped to his feet, the words escaping his lips in a kind of startled prayer. "The mountain! It's going to blow!"

"I told you," Hildy argued. "They took the signs and flags down."

"They was up a little while ago," he said. "Them fool kids musta stole 'em agin! Ye got to git outta here!"

Hildy instantly understood why the animated workmen sped off in the pickup. They must have realized the signs weren't up anymore and gone to get some more. Her heart pounded within her, but her anger overshadowed her fear. "I'm not leaving until you settle with me!" she said firmly. "Tell me. Don't you even care enough to at least see your own flesh and blood?"

He sighed and sat down on the wagon tongue. "I been all mixed up since I heard that some gal was a-lookin' fer me, claiming we was kin. But I didn't believe it. I didn't want to believe it!"

"Why not?"

"Why not?" The man's voice rose in anguish. "Look at me! I've wasted my life. Failed at everything. After Beulah'n me split—I never knew she was a-fixin' to have no baby—I started driftin' and drinkin'. I was mostly a saddle-tramp cowboy. But I finally sunk so low nobody'd let me ride fer 'em."

He wiped his eyes with the back of his dirty hand. "Bought me a little ranch, but I failed at that, too. Took out a loan but couldn't repay it. I got so desprit I couldn't get no job 'cept herdin' sheep! Me, a cowboy, jist a sheepherder a-wantin' to die. But I was too weak to even do that, so I come over here, figgerin' the mountain'd do it fer me."

A chill swept Hildy as she understood what he meant. "You mean, you're deliberately waiting. . . ?"

He nodded. "I cain't take keer of myself. How could I take keer of a daughter?"

Hildy's anger slipped away, and she felt sudden compassion for her uncle. "Since you met Beulah at a camp meeting, you must believe in God," she said softly.

"Did, long time ago."

"He's still God, and He can help you change."

"Too late."

"You're still alive," Hildy reminded him. "So it's not too late!"

"Too late," he repeated, eyes downcast.

"Don't you care about anything? Your ranch?"

"Let Kessick have it. He holds the mortgage."

"I know, but . . . if anything happened to you, that ranch should rightfully belong to your daughter."

Nate Konning raised his eyes to meet Hildy's. "Never thought of that." He stood and looked straight at her. "I done one decent thing in life," he said. "In spite of drinkin' hard ever'time I got to town, I always saved somethin' ever' payday. Got some cash money hid at a secret place in The Pass behind my ranch.

"They's not enough to pay off the whole loan, but maybe she kin get Kessick to give her some time on the rest. I figgered I wouldn't need it when this mountain went, and Kessick'd never find it. Nobody would. I'll draw ye a map."

"That won't do!" Hildy protested. "The contract says you or your heir has to pay the note off today."

"I clean forgot that," her uncle said. "Me 'n Ozzie was a-jokin' when we wrote that about some heir, since I didn't have no kin."

"But you do have. A daughter. Are you still refusing—?"

"Hildy!" Spud's call interrupted her question.

Hildy glanced up to see the boy running toward her, and she sprinted in his direction. "What's wrong?"

Puffing from his run, Spud grabbed her shoulders. "Brother Ben just told me . . . that Ruby went off by herself up a little crack . . . by a lone pine on the mountain." He tried to catch his breath. "Figured she could see better from the top of that."

Nate Konning ran over to join the other two. "I know that crack!" he cried. "It's full of rattlers!"

Hildy spun to face her uncle. "You sure?"

"Positive. Must have a den in there."

Hildy whirled back to Spud. "Ruby's deathly afraid of snakes! We've got to stop her before she sees them and panics."

"Brother Ben tried to stop her," Spud told them, "but she wouldn't listen. Said she had to find her daddy." He stopped and blinked as though aware of the herder for the first time. "Are you Nate Konning?"

"Yes, he is," Hildy said. "Talk later! Come on!" She grabbed Spud's hand. "We've got to help Ruby!"

She and Spud had run a few steps toward Thunder Mountain when Hildy glanced back. Nate Konning still stood in the same spot. As Hildy watched, he turned away.

I can't believe it! she thought. *Turning his back on his only daughter.*

She and Spud raced past the place where they'd split up earlier. Spud led the way against the very base of the great mountain. Hildy followed him up a narrow ledge that slanted upward past a series of small recessed places. They reminded Hildy of cliffs she'd seen by the roadway.

Brother Ben was waiting for them at the bottom of the crack in the basalt by the lone pine. Barely two feet wide, the crack slanted upward like a rude trail made of small rocks and dirt that had slid down.

"It's okay," the old ranger said as Hildy and Spud slid to a halt, panting for air. "She's turned around and starting back down."

"I seed snakes!" Ruby cried, her voice shaking.

With Brother Ben on one side and Spud on the other, Hildy anxiously watched her cousin half-sliding, half-walking down the steep incline.

Suddenly, Spud stiffened. "Listen! What was that?"

Hildy glanced down, expecting to see a rattlesnake at their feet. But Spud wasn't looking down. His head cocked, he was listening intently.

"Whistles!" Spud whispered loudly. "And somebody shouting. Hear it?"

Hildy started to shake her head, then stopped in sudden, cold horror.

From a great distance came a man's hoarse cry. "Fire in the hole!"

Brother Ben quickly turned to the other two. "That's the powder monkey's yell, meaning she's going to blow!" he cautioned. "Spud, see if you can find any place for us to hide." The old ranger turned back to Ruby and yelled, "Slide! Do it now! They're going to dynamite this place!"

Hildy froze. Then suddenly she felt a strong hand grip her from behind. At first she thought it was Spud, but when she tore her eyes away from Ruby's last few feet of her tumbling slide, she looked directly into the unshaven face of Nate Konning.

"Quick!" he warned. "Take these and get back under that cave-like place over there! The rest of you, too!"

"But—" Hildy protested, glancing at the two short lengths of stovepipe Nate had shoved into her hands.

"Now!"

His voice cracked with such urgency that Hildy turned and ran for the overhanging shelter a short distance away. It was somewhat like a big letter *V* turned on its side. The open end flared out and up. It wasn't more than fifteen feet high and twenty feet wide at the front, ten deep and eight feet high at the back wall. All three walls were riddled with ground squirrel holes.

Hildy reached the recess two steps ahead of Spud and the old ranger. Still unconsciously clutching the two lengths of stovepipe, she stopped to look back at Ruby.

About thirty feet away, Ruby jumped up from her slide in a swirl of dry dust. Terror and revulsion showed in her eyes. "They's rattlers all—"

Nate Konning yelled to his daughter through cupped hands. "Jump into that little cave in front of you! Now!"

"But—"

"Do it now! Now!"

At the urgency of his voice, Ruby obeyed. She bent over and plunged into the hollow. Hildy couldn't see how deep it was but guessed it was so small that Ruby couldn't stand up.

Nate Konning spun and shoved Hildy back hard. "You get inside, too."

With the stovepipes in her arms, she staggered against the cool back wall and dropped the pipes. They rolled with a clatter against the back wall. She whirled and saw Spud, Brother Ben, and Nate Konning pressing against the wall beside her.

All of a sudden Hildy heard a loud "whump!" in the distance. It was instantly followed by another and another, each coming closer.

A second later, there was an explosion high overhead followed by a heavy rumble.

Avalanche! she thought.

She felt someone grip her hand hard and glanced to see Spud pushing her behind him. From the other side, the old ranger did the same as the first great boulders shot past the open shelter.

When the sound of explosions died, Nate Konning started toward the opening. Just then a great mass of dislodged rocks thundered past in a black cascade.

"Oh, Lord!" Hildy heard the trembling prayer even above the sliding, grinding, rushing roar of the mountain's collapsing face. Then she realized she wasn't *hearing* the prayer. She was *saying* it silently, over and over.

She broke it off when, through the dust, she realized that not more than four feet of light showed at the opening, and even that was closing. Some of the debris clattered inside the recess.

"We'll be buried alive!" Hildy cried, scrambling to her feet. Three pairs of hands grabbed her and dragged her back. She crouched with the others against the back wall, worrying about Ruby as a horrible roar engulfed them.

After what seemed forever, the incredible rumbling faded away. The stream of debris slowed to a trickle. A few rocks still shot by, barely visible through the choking dust.

As it settled, Hildy shook debris from herself and stood up with Spud and the two men. "We're alive!" she cried. "But . . . Ruby?"

Fearfully, she scrambled up the mass of loose black rocks that had almost filled the recess. Her hands were cut and bleeding, but she didn't care. Eagerly, she shoved her face through the small opening. Spud and the two men rushed to her side.

They all pushed rocks aside and slid through the opening. Hildy glanced toward Ruby's smaller shelter. It was piled high with debris. She started running across the tumbled mass of black rocks, but Nate Konning passed her.

He scrambled forward, half-falling, half-staggering in the still-shifting rocks, toward the place he had told Ruby to take shelter. Suddenly, he froze. "Wait!" He pointed ahead. "Listen!"

There was a furious buzzing directly ahead. Hildy's blood seemed to freeze in her body. "Rattlers! But where?" she whispered.

"In them ground squirrel holes an' under what's left of the other ledges," her Uncle Nate said. "Here they come! They're powerful mad! Stand still!"

Hildy shuddered and obeyed, remembering how fearful Ruby was of the poisonous creatures. But was she safe?

"Ooooh!" The moan came from somewhere ahead.

Hildy's eyes darted over to the opening of the smaller recess. Ruby was crawling over the rocks and debris that had nearly closed her shelter.

"She's hurt!" Hildy exclaimed. "Her head! See?"

"Ruby, stay there!" Brother Ben shouted.

The bleeding girl kept moving out onto the pile of rocks.

"She must not hear you!" Hildy cried.

"May have a concussion," Spud said. "She's certainly dazed. Look at her eyes."

"Ruby, stay there!" Hildy yelled. "There are rattlers between you and us!"

Ruby didn't seem to hear. She reached her hand up to her bloody scalp, then collapsed.

Hildy turned to face Spud and Brother Ben. "What'll we do?"

Nate Konning roughly pushed her aside and ran on uncertain legs back the way they'd come.

"Where's he going?" Spud demanded.

Hildy's heart sank. A few minutes before, she had seen Nate Konning arrive with the stovepipes. In that moment, Hildy thought he had changed his mind about seeing his daughter. His quick thinking had saved Ruby's life, and probably the others', too. But now Ruby was hurt, unconscious, and threatened by the very thing she feared most. And her father was running away!

Hildy shoved her disbelief and anger aside. Someone had to save her cousin. Hildy concentrated on the scene before her.

Three large snakes had oozed out of holes and were rattling furiously. One was about six feet in front of Hildy, coiled and warning her back. The second was slightly beyond, but the third was only a few feet in front of her cousin.

Hildy cried out. "Brother Ben, that one's starting toward Ruby!"

Spud reached down and picked up a recently dislodged rock, but the old ranger stopped him. "You might hit Ruby or make things worse!"

"Then what can we do?" the boy demanded. "We can't just leave her—"

He stopped and all three turned at a strange clattering sound behind them. Nate Konning slid down the pile of debris in stocking feet, his boots in his hands. On his calves he wore two new pieces of black stovepipe.

He quickly brushed the soles of his feet and began putting on his boots. "Learned this from a crazy trout fisherman," he explained, forcing the metal pipe down over the high topped boots. "Let's hope it works as well as he said it did."

"What in the world. . . ?" Hildy asked as her uncle clumped by, heading straight for his daughter.

"Look out!" Spud yelled.

Too late! The nearest reptile's ugly head struck at Nate's right leg. There was a dull thud against the metal, and twin streams of a nearly clear liquid slid down the stovepipe.

Hildy started to feel sick.

Nate Konning turned his head and half smiled at them. Then he kept going.

Hildy held her breath as the other snakes struck. Nate Konning didn't even slow down. In a few seconds, he reached his daughter and bent over her.

Ruby stirred and raised her head. For a moment, she didn't seem to realize where she was. Then she saw the snakes and frantically scrambled backward. Her father grabbed her and lifted her into his arms.

"I'm . . . skeered!" Ruby screeched.

"It's okay," Nate said with awkward tenderness. "Yore safe now."

Ruby looked up into his eyes. "Who . . . who air ye?"

"I'm yore daddy," he replied. "An' I'm a-carin' fer ye same's any daddy would fer his child. Now ye jist rest easy while I walk us back through them critters. Then we ain't never goin' to be apart no more!"

Hot tears filled Hildy's eyes. She was barely able to see when Nate Konning passed the last danger. He set Ruby on her feet by Spud and Brother Ben.

Hildy impulsively reached up and grabbed both father and daughter in a sobbing embrace.

Nate bent down and whispered in her ear. "Reckon a feller kin change," he said, "with God's help, anyway. So I'd be obliged if ye fergit what I said a spell back."

"There's nothing to forget," Hildy whispered back. "Nothing at all!"

———

Late the following Sunday afternoon after everyone had gone home from the celebration at the barn-house, Hildy felt so good she thought she might burst. Just before five o'clock that Friday afternoon, Nate Konning paid off the mortgage with the money he had hidden away and a small loan from Ben Strong.

The widow Benton and her family were allowed to stay on in the sod house until Nate and his new-found daughter decided what they wanted to do. Meanwhile, the Konnings stayed with the Corrigans, sleeping on old coats and blankets in the west end of the barn-house where there was plenty of room.

Mischief had been gone a month, but the night before the celebration, a boy from a couple miles away showed up with the coon in his arms. "My dog treed her a few weeks back," he explained. "I penned her up, figuring to keep her as my pet. Then yesterday I found one of your signs, and, well . . . she's yours again."

Joe Corrigan still hadn't found a car to replace the one that was smashed, but he was borrowing a neighbor's for a while. Somehow, Hildy believed that was going to work out, too.

Hildy kept remembering Brother Ben's warning about guarding her thoughts, and having a purpose, a plan, and lots of perseverance.

Later that afternoon she and Spud walked along the Ladino clover fence, watching the sun set. "I'm going to start planning how to get our 'forever' home, and not just talk about it," she determined. "And I'm going to persevere until we get it, just as Ruby did in finding her father."

Spud smiled. " 'As a man thinks in his heart, so is he,' " he quoted. "I believe you're thinking right, Hildy."

"How about you, Spud? Written your mother yet?"

"No, but I'll do it right away," he promised.

Hildy looked across the barnyard to where Ruby was walking with her father, their arms around each other. "I see God working in all our lives," she said softly. "I wonder what He's going to do next?"

"I don't know, but I want to see it happen."

Hildy grinned. "So do I," she said. "So do I."